STALKER

A novel by
Natalie Kaye Saar

Acknowledgments

I started to make a list of all of the people I need to thank, but then I realized I'd need another book for that. So, I'll keep it brief.

None of this could be possible without God, so that's first and foremost.

Thank you to my parents, Jim and Sheri, who instead of laughing at me when I said I wanted to be a writer, supported me without question.

Thank you to my siblings Nicole, Noelle, JP, and Drew who constantly inspire me to be great, because I have to keep up with them.

Thank you to Brad La Pointe and Caitlin Schulz for keeping me motivated and for picking me up off the floor every time I broke down crying when I realized there are millions of other authors out there.

Thank you to my Aunt Lori, Megan Mann, Taylor Martindale, and Ashley Levine for your invaluable advice and support, without which, this book wouldn't have happened.

Thank you to my Nana and Grandma who have loved everything I've written, even if it was in crayon.

Thank you to my high school English teachers Mr. Jeff Hauge and Mrs. Pat Heckert for helping me realize my passion for writing, and the confidence to chase that dream.

And a very big thank you to all of my friends and family. You all have touched my life in some way, and urged me to continue on, whether you realize it or not.

Calle Pompeii was a street like any other in modern day Suburbia. The men jogged with their playful dogs, and the women walked to the park with their baby strollers. The postman promptly delivered the mail every day and the newsboy always had the papers out early. It was a place where people said 'Hi' to each other in passing. Little did they know that their daily routines were being watched.

Missy was the first one in their neighborhood to become a victim.

She was a nanny for the Richards family. Mr. Richards worked for a local software company and his wife stayed home with the kids. There was no reason for Mrs. Richards to need a nanny, but she somehow convinced her husband that she needed help. She couldn't take care of her children on her own, but oddly enough, her nanny found a way to make it a one-woman job. Missy loved the children, Ben and Franny.

Ben was five years old and loved to play at the park. Franny was four years old and wanted to be just like her brother, so, of course she loved the park too. Ben and Franny were a bit of an oddity when it came to siblings, because they liked to play together instead of fighting like brothers and sisters usually do. Missy would always tell her friends that they were the easiest kids she'd ever nannied for; so easy in fact that she could do it while being high... The entire time.

Meanwhile, Mrs. Richards was too busy trying to shoddily hide her affair with the gardener to notice that her nanny was completely stoned. She'd hurry Missy off to the park, with Ben and Franny in tow, as soon at Jorge's truck pulled up.

Missy had to hand it to Mrs. Richards, if she was going to have an affair, at least she was doing it with a smokin' hot guy. Jorge had abs rippling on his abs. It was a beautiful sight.

Milton documented all this in his notebook. He'd been following Missy for about four months. She hadn't noticed his presence even once. Maybe it was the weed, or maybe it was that he'd been stalking people for decades and had never been caught.

~~~

The first time Milton spied on someone, other than his mother, he was so nervous that he pissed himself. Each time after that it came more and more naturally to him. He would find the subject and follow her, writing down all of her daily activities in a journal.

It was like writing down observations in a science

experiment; everything was important. From what the subject ate for breakfast to when the subject slept; Milton needed to document it. He'd know when his time was up with a subject because his journal would be full with observations. Once a journal was full of information about a person, it was time for him to get rid of the subject. Forever.

Missy only had a month's worth of pages left in her journal; her time was ticking down and she had no idea.

Milton looked at her, sitting there on the swings, watching Ben and Franny play tag on the jungle gym. He made a note in his journal about what she was wearing.

Ruffle blouse with a revealing neckline. Minorly see through. Tight jeans. Butt crack is visible when she is sitting. She doesn't seem to notice. He noted.

A long time ago, Milton learned that his journals last longer if he used all of the space on every line, instead of stopping at the designated red lines. His notes were barely distinguishable in terms of time and coherency, but *he* knew what they meant. He'd read them so many times that his note taking skills had been perfected over the years.

At first, Milton used the regular composition notebooks from the store for his journals — the black and white kind they make you get in school. After his first subject, he realized that these lasted for too short of a time. The lines were too thick and he didn't get long enough to know her before her time was up. So, he switched to large 11.5" x 8" college ruled multi-subject notebooks. These were hard to find, so when he did, he bought as many as there were in the store. One time, he bought 53. When the cashier looked at him like he was crazy, he hastily said he was a teacher.

Time went on and Milton found himself writing smaller and smaller so that he could write even more. However, if he'd spent some time with a girl, and decided he didn't like her, he would write larger to make the time go faster.

Giving up before the book was finished was not an option. Milton *had* to finish the whole thing, then get her out of his life, though the journal would remain with him forever.

Franny screamed and Milton looked up, not at the child but at Missy. He had to document how she would react to the hollering kid. Missy walked slowly over to Franny.

"What's wrong Franny Bananny?" Missy said.

"Ben pushed me. I have a boo boo." Franny made a pouty face and held her tiny scratched elbow to the nanny's face. Missy looked to Ben.

"Ben, did you push her?" Ben made a petulant frown; the kind where a child poutily purses his lips and crosses his arms in front of his chest.

Then Ben looked at Franny's big, glassy eyes, while she clung to Missy for dear life. Ben's guilt won and his look softened. He ran over to Franny with his arms wide open, implying he wanted a hug.

"Yes. I pusheded her. I'm sowwy Fwanny." Ben still couldn't speak perfectly, much to his mother's chagrin. He hugged Franny and the sadness was instantly erased from her face. She smiled and happily said, "It's okay Ben! I fo'give you."

The duo resumed their game of tag, and Missy resumed eating the brownie that was in her pocket. Milton watched as she walked back to the swing on which she had been sitting.

Subject is preoccupied with getting stoned by eating a brownie. Gained approximately five pounds in the last month. Muffin top visible over pants.

Any detail, no matter how minute, was important.

Missy's back was to Milton, and she had no idea he was there. The stalker sat on a blanket, neatly hidden in the bushes behind her. His operation was so streamlined that no one would have the slightest idea he was watching them. For hours he sat and watched Missy, never tiring, losing focus or taking his eyes off of her. He just sat, watching her sit. Sometimes she would get up and throw a ball back to the kids if it came near her, but mostly she just sat.

~~~

Looking down at her watch, Missy realized it was 4 o'clock. She had to get Ben and Franny back and make dinner before Mr. Richards got home. Mrs. Richards should be done with her afternoon 'workout' by now.

Missy had made the mistake of coming back to the house too early one time. Franny had puked on the playground and needed to go home and get cleaned up. After entering the house, Missy could hear what sounded like a scream, and immediately she was alarmed. Then, she heard a male grunting in the same direction of the scream. Cautiously, Missy backed out of the house right as Mrs. Richards climaxed. Missy hurried the children back out of the house, *looking flustered and appalled*, according to Milton's journal, *but handled the situation well.*

4 o'clock should be fine. Missy rounded up the two kids, whose energy was waning anyway. Little Franny playfully collapsed on the way home. "I'm too tired. Carry me!" She reached her hands up to Missy. There was no way to say no to that cute mess of curly hair. Missy picked Franny up and started carrying her. Then Ben collapsed. "Me too Missy! I'm ti-yed." Missy was too high for this shit.

"Okay Ben, how about I carry Franny to the street sign, then give you a piggy back ride. Franny you think you could walk so your brother can rest a little?"

Franny looked at her brother sprawled on the sidewalk and took pity. "Okay, I can walk."

Ben jumped up off the ground and ran to the next street sign. Missy readjusted Franny and kept on walking. When she got to the sign she slid one child off her back and pulled the other one up.

~~~

Milton hung back behind the group far enough to avoid being noticed, but close enough to hear what they were saying.

He found a quiet comfort in these suburban towns that he didn't have elsewhere. In cities, there are millions of people, but those same people are often much more alert and aware of their surroundings as a result. They'll take note of a man who is staring at them, even if he is doing it innocently. Once he's seen, he's doomed. It's only a matter of time until that man is reported to the authorities, which no one wants.

In the suburbs, people see each other doing the same activity every single day. Since their schedules are more predictable, people are less aware of their surroundings because they seemingly never change. From a quick glance, everything was as it should be, and that's all that mattered. Besides, no one wanted to believe their perfect little town could have any kind of danger lurking.

Milton knew he was sick, that there was something wrong with his mind, but he didn't know what to do about it. More importantly, he didn't know how to control it. He'd been this way for so long and had never been caught, so he didn't feel a need to get any help. Besides, the help he got as a teen was painful and worthless.

Milton followed Missy and the kids to the Richards' house. Just as they arrived, he saw the gardener's truck driving down the street. He'd seen enough affairs to know what this was, but he just checked his watch and noted it in the journal; no judgment.

Gardener leaving the house. Obvious affair taking place. Missy may have noticed since they returned later than usual.

Missy trailed the kids into the house. Once the door was closed and locked, Milton walked into a small, shrubbed area at the front of the house. There were large windows at the front which exposed the clean, fancy family room to the public street. It was the kind with sleek white couches and gold accents everywhere. No one would ever guess that children lived here. Milton could see the two kids sitting on the couch, shoes off and looking exhausted. Missy brought them each a glass of water and turned on a movie for them.

The Jungle Book. Third time this week. He noted.

Throwing a blanket over Ben and Franny, Missy went to the kitchen to get dinner started, and to smoke. Milton knew that she made dinner around this time, so he sat back, waiting for her to reappear after she made whatever it was she was cooking tonight. By the time Missy came back with two trays, the children had regained their energy. Milton pulled a pocket-sized pair of binoculars from his coat and peered at the kids' TV trays of food.

Macaroni and cheese with broccoli. Apple juice. He noted.

~~~

Missy sat down next to them with a bowl of her own macaroni and broccoli. She tricked herself into thinking it was healthy by adding broccoli. Lately, Missy had noticed that the pounds had been piling on, but with this full time nannying gig she was too busy to exercise. She'd just have to put more broccoli in with the macaroni. Or something. "That should do the trick," she thought to herself.

The best, and worst, part of being a nanny was that Missy had endless access to food. Mrs. Richards never ate, and Mr. Richards couldn't care less about the food inventory in his home — that was a woman's job, according to him — so Missy ate and ate.

Mrs. Richards came down the stairs while the three of them were enjoying the meal. She was in a short, tight, red cocktail dress that left nothing to the imagination, along with sky-high heels, and was putting some large faux-diamond earrings through her pierced earlobes.

"Has my husband come home yet?" she asked absently.

"No Mrs. Richards, not yet," Missy replied, trying to

seem sober. Not that it mattered; Mrs. Richards rarely looked her in the eye.

"Well, tell him I went on ahead to the dinner. The reservation is in our name and I can't keep our guests waiting."

"No problem Mrs. Richards. I'll make sure he knows."

Ben and Franny were mesmerized by the movie and didn't even notice their gorgeous mom. She walked over to them and gave them each a fake kiss on the top of their heads. Mrs. Richards had already carefully applied her dark red lipstick, so she wasn't about to *actually* kiss her kids.

"Bye babies. I'll see you when I get home tonight."

"Bye mama," they said in unison, unenthused. Missy was more of a mom to them than their own mother. They cried when Missy left, but not when Mrs. Richards did.

~~~

Mrs. Richards left the house, looking like a 25-year-old on the way to a night out with the girls. Milton watched her leave, because it was impossible not to. The way she swayed her hips when she walked, and the way that her dress hugged every curve, it was hard to look away.

The sun was setting, and the adulteress was driving off into it. Soon, it would be completely dark, save the circles of light that the streetlights threw onto the pavement. That was Milton's least and most favorite time of the day. He didn't have to worry about people sneaking up on him or seeing him, however he did have to worry about wild animals catching him off guard. Ever prepared, Milton always carried a bottle of mace with him, just in case he was attacked. The chance was slim, but one can never be too careful.

Missy knelt down in front of the kids once their mom was gone. "Who wants ice cream?" she asked them. Both of their faces lit up and they yelled. She ushered them into the kitchen. Milton couldn't hear what she was saying once she was in the house, but he'd become quite an amazing lip reader over the years. He could also read body language with the skill of someone who had a PhD in the subject. Unfortunately, Missy's back was to him right now.

Just as the nanny started leading the kids to the kitchen, Mr. Richards pulled into the driveway. He got out of the car with some difficulty, due to the fact that he was obese. Not morbidly obese, but just that side of overweight. He could have used some more broccoli in his macaroni too. He grabbed his briefcase and lumbered into the house.

When Mr. Richards walked in the door he got a much different response than his wife. "Sports fans, I'm home!" he yelled. The kids came running up to him, arms wide open. "Daddy!" they yelled. Missy stood in the doorway to the kitchen. Her silhouette highlighted by the light behind her; to Milton she looked angelic.

The light accentuates every one of her curves, even the muffin top, he flatly noted.

~~~

Once Mr. Richards had finished hugging the kids, they ran back into the kitchen and Missy followed. "Hello Missy, how're you today?" the man of the house said to her, forcing her to hang back for a moment.

Missy answered shyly, "I'm good Mr. Richards. Your wife said to tell you that she didn't want to be late and went ahead to the dinner."

"Oh, she did? Well, I'll follow behind her in a bit. What's for dinner *here*?"

Missy looked surprised. "Oh I didn't know you'd be joining us. I'd have made something with meat in it for you."

"I've had enough *meat* for the day," he said.

Missy ignored his vulgar tone. "I made the kids macaroni and cheese with broccoli. They'll only eat their greens if they're mixed into something else, and this is their favorite."

"It looks good to me," he said, not looking her in the eye, but looking lower.

Uncomfortable, Missy went to the stove and spooned some cheesy pasta shells onto a plate for him. He sat down at the table next to his kids. "So what did you three do today?" he asked the kids as Missy put a plate of food in front of him.

"We went to the park!" Franny said.

"Oh you did? What did you do there?"

"We played games!" Ben said. "Daddy do you want to come with us tomorrow?"

Mr. Richards smiled and talked with his kids, an air of arrogance in his voice. "I'm very busy tomorrow Benny Boy. I have to work to put this food on the table," he said, rubbing the table.

The children were crestfallen and he noticed. "Maybe we can all go to the park this weekend," the suggested. They perked right back up.

"Yeah!" the kids yelled in unison. Their plates were empty and they walked them to the sink where Missy was standing, handing her the dirty dishware.

"I'm going to take a shower," Ben yelled. He was inexplicably excited about everything. It didn't matter what it was, Ben was going to find a way to be ecstatic about it. Even chores.

"I want to play house. Missy you be the mommy and I be the baby," Franny said.

Apparently, Franny thought she was *so* much older than a baby. Missy laughed briefly at this request then agreed. Franny ran out of the room to get in her crib, which was actually the crib for her babydolls since she'd outgrown it. This left Missy and Mr. Richards alone in the kitchen. He got up from the table and walked to the sink, holding his plate out in front of him. He got very close to Missy; so close that his protruding belly was almost touching her.

"Here you go little Missy," he breathed at her, with stale cheesy broccoli breath.

"Thank you," she stiffly and tentatively took the plate and began to jerkily wash it.

Mr. Richards moved away from Missy, but she could feel his eyes at her back. She hurriedly did the dishes and placed them haphazardly in the dish rack . "I'm coming Franny," she yelled after the girl and walked out of the kitchen. Mr. Richards watched her go past him as she went. He then trudged upstairs too, with a reluctant gait.

~~~

Joining his wife was the last thing Mr. Richards wanted to do. In actuality, the dinner didn't start for another hour, but he knew why she'd left early. She liked to hit the bar before these types of engagements, because she loved attention and she always got it when she went out by herself. He wasn't home enough to give his wife what she needed, but he also had to work 60 hours a week to support *her* lifestyle. It was a catch-22, but clearly the better move was to stay together for the kids, and because his wife had a nice ass.

When the Richardses met, they'd been very much in love. She had a tight body, he was in the best shape of his life, and they'd had a lot of fun together. Then she got pregnant, he bought a house with a white picket fence, and everything had slowly gone to shit. He was lucky if they had sex once every other week.

Since the day they'd hired Missy, Mr. Richards liked her. She reminded him of how his wife used to be, not the slut she'd turned into. He'd divorce her eventually, but he didn't want his kids to grow up without a mother... and he didn't want to have to give her child support if the courts didn't vote in his favor. No, it was clearly smarter to endure her for another 15 years until the kids were grown up and off at college.

In the meantime, he had Missy to keep him happy, and he fully planned to seduce her. Sure, he wasn't in as good of shape as he used to be when he was a young man, but he had money, and that had proven to be enough to get any woman so far.

~~~

Missy was playing "house" with Franny. Basically she was doing the same thing she did all day, but in Mrs. Richards' patronizing voice; Franny liked it because she got to talk even more like a baby than she already did.

"Mama, baybay," Franny said, pointing to a fake bottle nearby.

"You want a bottle baby Fran Fran?" Missy said while reaching for the bottle.

"Gimme gimme mama!" Franny motioned for the bottle while still laying in her makeshift crib. It was constructed of blankets and pillows. Ben built castles out of these plush decorations, but Franny preferred cribs.

"Okay baby Franny. Here you go!" she handed the baby the bottle.

Missy couldn't wait for Mr. Richards to leave so she could get high again. She was all too sober to be playing "house" right now.

Ben came bounding down the stairs. He'd wrapped his towel around his neck, like a cape, and was standing at the top of the stairs in all of his birthday suit glory. "I'm supaman!" he proudly announced, putting his hands on his hips.

Missy and Franny giggled. They both got up. "Let's go help Superman find his clothes," Missy told Franny.

"Mama wants him to wear his pajamas. I'll show you where they are," bossy Franny said as she took Missy's hand and led her upstairs.

As Missy trudged up, she had to walk past the beaming eyes of Mr. Richards. He always made her feel so uncomfortable, but she was too poor to quit this job. It had taken her months to find any kind of employment and she knew she'd never be able to get another one before rent was due. She followed Franny into Ben's room and watched her pull out the pajamas that Ben was supposed to wear, according to his mother. They was a two-piece pajama set with his favorite cartoon character on it. What Mrs. Richards lacked in being a mother, she felt that she made up for in the things she bought for his kids.

Mr. Richards came into the room. "I'll be heading out now. The dinner should be starting soon, and I'm sure my wife will start to worry." He looked to Franny. "You'll be good for Missy, right?"

Franny smiled at her dad. "Yes daddy. I'll be good." He smiled back. Then looked to Missy.

"You be good too," he said, and winked.

Missy gave a half-hearted, nervous laugh. He left the room and her demeanor instantly changed. She was relaxed and playful with Franny again. Ben got out of the shower and got dressed, the Franny hopped in the tub. Missy was paranoid about anything bad happening to the kids, so she made sure to play games nearby with Ben while Franny was in the tub. Mr. and Mrs. Richards were the type of people who would sue her, accuse her of negligence and imprison her if any harm were ever to come to their children, though they probably left their kids in the tub for hours when she wasn't around.

So, Missy made sure to always be attentive, even when she was high.

~~~

While Missy was upstairs with the children, Milton would read a book, review his journal, or sneak around, trying to get a better glimpse of Missy. When she was upstairs though, this was nearly impossible. There were no giant trees to climb onto and nowhere he could inconspicuously put up a ladder. There was one thing he could use though.

The Richards' had a backyard that made the sneaking on the ground fairly easy. Their house sat in a corner, on a hill so that no one could see into their yard. This made it very easy for Mrs. Richards to tan in the nude around the same time the pool boy came over. It was coincidence, of course.

There was a wooden patio cover right below the master bedroom window. Milton would climb up onto the top of the patio cover, using the tables and furniture outside. He couldn't see Missy clearly through the bedroom window, but he could catch glimpses of her when she was playing with the children.

Playing with toy cars in the hallway with Ben. Is looking tired, but is keeping up with the kids. He noted.

This was Milton's least favorite part of the day. It was hard to stalk someone when he couldn't see them. He couldn't write down valuable specific details about Missy, like how she handled the kids and how they responded to her. He needed to know little intricacies about her. Her being trapped in a house made that hard to do.

It was cold on this particular night, so Milton decided to crawl off the patio cover and go back to his car. He'd parked across the street from the house, where he had been for the past few weeks. During the day, it was possible for people to see him sitting there, which is why he preferred bushes when the sun was out, but at night, it was much harder to see someone in a car. The only thing that could have given him away were the fogged up windows that drew curiosity. Once they got cloudy, he bundled up and left for the bushes again. He made sure to only stay in the car long enough so that the windows didn't fog up, because he couldn't see inside with hazy windows anyway.

Milton had to look through the front window to see Missy in the house. She didn't do much during the night after the kids went to sleep. Just watched TV, cleaned up and got smoked. The usual. This was easily the most boring part of his day, and he loathed it, but he couldn't leave, no matter the weather and no matter how bored he got. He had to stay and watch Missy. He had to learn her patterns and document them. He'd try and infer why she did what she did, and the way she went about doing things. In fact, Milton had been following her so long that he knew more about her than she knew about herself.

He saw himself as a modern-day Darwin discovering the creatures of the Galapagos; only in Milton's case he was discovering the way humans *actually* acted when they thought no one was watching them, and this suburbia was his tropical island.

There were lots of intimate things Milton learned about his subjects because he followed them so closely. For example, he knew that Missy's favorite number was 13, she liked the color red and her favorite animal was the giraffe.

He knew that she'd recently been dumped by a guy she liked because she was too boring. That's not what the guy told her, but rather what Milton had deduced from the situation, since he'd been able to hear a few of her phone calls.

Milton knew that Missy liked her mom, but not her dad, since he left them when she was young. He knew that her best friend was sleeping with Missy's ex, and Missy had lied saying that it was okay with her. *She'd rather lie than lose a friend*. Milton knew that she ate brownies when she missed her ex, not the "special brownies," just regular old feel-good brownies, like Mom made before Dad ruined everything. She ate Popsicles when she was feeling happy, and at peace with her life. He knew that she wanted to be a teacher because she liked working with kids; little kids, not older know-it-alls. Most importantly, Milton knew that Missy had no direction in life, no strong support system of people who really knew her, except for him. He was the best thing that had ever happened to her, "she just doesn't know it yet," he'd always think to himself. Milton was waiting for the best time to tell Missy, but it just wasn't right yet. He'd have to finish the journal first, to make sure everything was complete, and then he could tell her. He had a very particular way of telling his subjects the things he had learned about them.

~~~

Every subject of Milton's got their own special journal, which he'd fill up with facts about the people, and his observations of their behavior. After finishing a journal, Milton would read through and study the notes he had taken on the person. Then, he'd compile everything he had learned about the subject's personality and really let her, or him, have it. Milton would tell his subjects everything. Every single brutal honesty about the person, which included both the good and bad.

Missy had her faults, but overall there were many more good characteristics than bad, which was not always the case. Milton found that you learn the most about someone by seeing what he or she does when they are alone, when no one is supposed to be watching. This is when people's true colors show.

Missy wasn't a bad person when she was alone, she just wasn't a very good one either. She didn't really do things for others, or volunteer, or do anything except for smoke, eat and watch TV. She didn't appear to have any goals or want to do anything ambitious. She started training for a half marathon, but when her boyfriend broke up with her, she decided she didn't want to do anything for three hours, let alone run. She really was just your average, everyday twenty-something girl, living life without any concern for the future or thought of anyone but herself. Milton watched her go through the motions of the rest of her night at the Richards' home.

~~~

The kids fell asleep on the couch and Missy walked them up to their rooms. She cleaned the kitchen, tidied up the living room and watched TV until the Richardses got home. Missy normally fell asleep quickly but tonight there was too much on her mind. She was trying to figure out her next move.

When Jay had broken up with Missy, he'd told her it was because of her lack of ambition, whatever the hell that meant. She didn't want him back, necessarily, she just wanted to prove him wrong. Normally she didn't care about a guy leaving her, but Jay was different. She had really thought he was "the one."

Missy figured that Jay had been "the one" for her, but she wasn't for him, which is why she had to 'get some ambition.' She had to prove her ex wrong and rub her success in his smug face. This wouldn't be easy though, mostly because she had no idea what she wanted to do. She decided to make a list of things she was good at:
Cooking (only easy stuff like pasta)
Making conversation
Taking care of other people's children
Eating
Organizing (only other people's stuff)
Getting high
Sleeping

That's all she could come up with.

In college, Missy's major was "Liberal Arts" which was collegiate jargon for "A Lot of Random Shit." She didn't remember a thing, and her degree hadn't helped her find a job, or even figure out a career path. Coming out of college she realized that in this day and age, B.A.s are like high school degrees; they're a dime a dozen.

Missy kept thinking about what it was that she wanted, and at this stage in life, what she *needed* to do. She came up with nothing, as she tidied up the Richards' giant house. She stopped, looked around and thought to herself, "I'll never own a home at this rate."

It was that awkward moment in life where it hits you, "I'm not good at anything; there's nothing I do that is better than anyone else." It was a painful realization, but Missy had gotten there, and she began to cry right there on the couch.

~~~

Milton saw her crying through the window.

She starts crying after writing on a piece of paper. He noted.

It was one of those times Milton wished that he used spy equipment that could hear through wall so that he could know what was going on inside that house. But that stuff was always so clunky and obvious. Still, he needed to know why his subject was crying. Maybe he could even install a micro mic onto her backpack and hear everything all the time. He needed something to fill in the blanks missing in his journal. Missy's time was almost up and he hated the thought of having to dispose of her without knowing all the details.

This had happened to Milton a few times before: Jenny, Sara, Sasha, Linda; they had been a few of the women who he never got to really know as much as he'd liked. Their jobs made it difficult for him to hear what was going on at all times with them, up in those sky-high buildings. The time of year that he stalked people made a big difference too. During the summer, people left their windows open and it was easy to hear everything that was going on. The wintertime was tough though. Their windows were shut up tight and he could only observe.

While Milton knew he needed the extra equipment, there was a very slim chance of that happening. He didn't like carrying stuff that big around. It drew too much attention. Besides, if he was holding up some machine, he ran a greater risk of someone noticing him, however putting a microphone on Missy's backpack felt like too much of a violation of privacy. As long as he stayed outside the dwelling his subject was in, he was giving her all the personal space she needed.

"People need space and privacy," or so Milton was taught in the mental hospital. But his observations violated neither of those things. *Anyone* could look into a house or a setting at a public park, and that's all that he did; anything that other people could do too.

So, he sat, watching Missy cry, and being able to do nothing about it. Did she need a friend? Did she need advice? Milton didn't know, and it might never become clear.

~~~

Mr. Richards came home and found Missy asleep on the couch. He had left the dinner well before his wife did; in fact, she was probably going to be there for awhile. He had no desire to sit anymore though, watching her flirt with every man in his company who was just waiting for her tit to pop out of her dress. It was like watching a train wreck, and he wondered what happened to the woman he married. The woman who had eyes only for him and who couldn't wait to see him at the end of every day. He wanted that woman back, not this slut that threw herself at any man besides him. He told her that he was tired and was going home, that he had to leave early the next day.

The scorned husband thought about Missy the entire night and the whole drive home. When he saw her laying on the couch like that, he was completely conflicted. The half of him that hated his wife said to take the nanny, right then and there. His wife wouldn't be home for hours, so there was plenty of time, and he was *pretty* sure he'd seen Missy give him a look here and there. Then the humane side of him, the practical side, kicked in and he decided against violating this young girl. Instead he just announced his presence.

"Missy! I'm back."

Missy stirred to life, and was startled when she realized it was *just* Mr. Richards in the entryway, not Mrs. Richards. She hurriedly got her stuff together and then it hit her: he was going to have to take her home. "Mr. Richards, why are you back so early? Where's Mrs. Richards?" she said hastily, trying not to show the slight tremble in her voice.

"Oh I have an early day tomorrow and Mrs. Richards wanted to stay a bit longer."

"Gotcha. Well, since you have an early day tomorrow I

can just wait for Mrs. Richards to get home and drive me back to my apartment," Missy hoped he would go for this idea, but she knew better.

"No, it's fine, I'll drive you back. It won't be a problem at all," he said, with a skeevy smile spreading across his fat face.

Missy realized there was one last way to escape the dreaded car ride! "Oh, but Mr. Richards, who will stay with the children? You can't leave them unattended. Really, it's okay, I'll just wait for Mrs. Richards," Missy pleaded.

"Don't worry about them," he said, crushing Missy's hopes, "They'll be fine for a few minutes."

"Oh, but it'll be more than a few minutes. I live all the way back in the city," she tried again."

It didn't matter. He was eerily determined.

~~~

Mr. Richards was touched at how much Missy seemed to care for his children. "She would make a great mother," he thought to himself.

Maybe he could divorce his wife and run away with

her. "Missy, really, don't be so worried. What could happen? They're asleep right now. They'll be fine. Get your stuff and let's go."

As for the kids, they were asleep and wouldn't even notice they'd been left alone. Besides, he couldn't wait to be alone in the car with her. It's all he'd been thinking about all night, being alone with Missy like he was right now. Looking at her young, fertile body, with her wide hips. She clearly didn't care *too* much about her looks, so he figured she'd be willing to give him a few more children. Maybe even get started tonight, if things went his way.

He knew it was a long shot, but Mr. Richards had been a charmer his whole life. Even now, he could still get the ladies at work all hot and bothered, so making Missy fall in love with him didn't seem like too much of a stretch.

~~~

Missy reluctantly gathered her things together and Milton thought to himself again that he needed a way to hear through those walls. He could read Missy's body language because she was in the window, and she looked very uneasy, stepping back and leaning away from Mr. Richards. However, the man of the house was just out of Milton's line of sight, so he had no idea what was going on to make his subject feel so uncomfortable. Once Missy finished getting her stuff together, Milton slunk down in the seat of his car so that no one would see him.

He watched as Missy and Mr. Richards left the house. Hastily, and clumsily, he fumbled to open the door for her, but Missy rushed to not let it happen. Mr. Richards ended up just shutting the door, and drove out of the driveway in his upscale car. Milton started his car and trailed them with his lights off. It wasn't safe to turn them on yet. He would do that once he reached the more populated parts of town. Any half-aware person would spot a car with its lights on following them in this quiet neighborhood at this hour of the night.

They finally turned out on to the main streets. Once they neared the freeway Milton turned his lights on. There were very few people on the road which made it easy to follow them, but also to stay far enough behind to be unnoticed.

~~~

Inside the car, Missy was very tense. She didn't know what was going to happen. Nothing, she assumed, but she could smell alcohol on Mr. Richards' breath and he was starting to ask some personal questions.

"So Missy," he started, "When did you decide you

wanted to Nanny?"

She'd been working with his family for nearly a year so it seemed odd to be interviewed right now, but she drew out her answer nonetheless, because the quiet moments with him were the most unbearable.

"Well, I babysat for a few families all throughout high school and college. When I graduated, I had all the certifications to be a nanny, and no one was hiring in my field, so I decided to look for a job with a family. You were the first family I interviewed with."

"I see," Mr. Richards said. "And what field were you looking for a job in? What was your major in college?"

"I was a Liberal Arts major. I suppose I wanted to go into teaching and working with little kids, but was just never sure I could do it on a day-to-day basis. Those kids can be pretty hard to deal with."

"But you work with my kids daily?"

"Well, yeah, but that's different. There's only two of them, not 20, and besides, I love your kids. Ben and Franny are the most adorable children ever." Missy really did love working with Ben and Franny. They were pretty well-behaved, and Mrs. Richards didn't give a damn what Missy did on-the-job as long as her kids were happy, and semi-healthy.

Though, sometimes she felt sad that such awesome kids were stuck with the worst parents. These two deserved a fun-loving family that did things together, like family bike rides and game night. Though, if the Richardses were those types of parents, they wouldn't need a nanny.

~~~

That was what Mr. Richards wanted to hear. He knew that Missy would make the perfect mother for his kids. She already spent so much time with them anyway. He'd venture to guess that she knew more about his kids than their own mother did.

Then the awkward silence reared its ugly head again. Mr. Richards quickly filled it with the question he'd been dying to ask. "So do you have a boyfriend?"

~~~

Missy was about as far from having a boyfriend as a person could be. She was still completely heartbroken over losing Jay. They'd had such a strong connection that she was sure she'd never find again in a man. Unfortunately, when it came to talking about Jay, he was best described through experience rather than adjectives. While Missy and Jay were over for good, Missy felt that if she lied and told Mr. Richards about him as though they were still together, he would leave her alone, and she'd be taken back to a better time in her life. It was a win-win to pretend this time.

"Yes I do have a boyfriend, and he's amazing! His name is Jay and he's the sweetest guy in the whole world. On my birthday last year he had flowers delivered to me in every single class I had at college that day, then I got home and he'd filled my apartment with dozens of sunflowers, since those are my favorites. On our first date he took me to this quaint little Italian place which had tables that only seated two. He'd send me cards in the mail for no reason, just to surprise me when I went to my mailbox. In fact, we recently took a big step, and I gave him a key to my apartment. Now he surprises me with home-cooked meals all of the time," she gushed. That last bit about the cooking was untrue, but Missy knew that if they had gotten to that point in the relationship, then Jay would have done all of those sweet this for her, but she drove him away. Just like everyone else.

Besides, the relationship never even had a chance to get that far. Jay had done some of the sweet things in the past that Missy said he did, and she gave him hardly anything – emotionally – in return. She didn't know how to! He was one of those people who was constantly upbeat and positive, so there was never a need for Missy to give him anything emotionally. Or at least that's what she thought.

Losing Jay was so painful to think about that Missy started crying without realizing she was.

"He sounds like a great guy," Mr. Richards said, then he noticed her tears. "Are you okay, Missy?"

She quickly pulled herself together. "Yes, yes I'm fine, I just love him so much, ya know? When you love someone so much it hurts?" It was the best excuse she could think of in a pinch, and it wasn't really an excuse. Just the thought of losing Jay hurt her.

Missy once read that ending a romantic relationship had the same emotional effect on the body as when someone dies. This was bullshit as far as Missy was concerned, because at least when someone was dead you could remember them fondly. But when people broke up, they never wanted to think of what was lost ever again. She didn't, anyway.

~~~

"Yes I do," he said. In fact, Mr. Richards had no idea what it felt like to love someone so much that it hurt. When he met Mrs. Richards, she had been young and beautiful and he had been young and ambitious. It was a whirlwind romance and when he proposed to her, she said yes without thinking twice. He asked her more out of ritual, because they both knew they'd get married, more out of lust than love, which seemed ironic now. She was never the settling-down type, but he knew he'd need a piece of arm candy to accompany him to events, and she never wanted to work a day in her life. What he didn't plan on was getting overweight and his wife feeling the need to screw someone else who wasn't paying her bills.

"So how long have you two been together then?" Mr. Richards continued to question Missy. If she and her boyfriend weren't too serious, maybe he could persuade her to ditch this Jay guy, the same way he had with his wife.

~~~

"It's been about two years," Missy responded. That's what it would have been if she hadn't driven him away. In her fantasy, they'd have been married within two years and be living happily ever after in a big house. They'd have dinner parties with all of their friends, and people would whisper, "Aren't Missy and Jay just the cutest?!"

Instead Missy and Jay had lasted a mere six months,

and she'd been pining for him ever since. A year and a half to get over six months. Something was just not right about that, and she knew it, but she didn't know how to be herself again. With Jay, she'd been the best version of 'Missy' that she'd ever known.

~~~

"Well, that's not too long," Mr. Richards said. He needed to make her forget this boy. He was more of a man than Jay would ever be anyway.

Men didn't do that kind of sweet stuff for women; only boys had the time to think about doing all of those things. "I am a real man," Mr. Richards told himself. He had two kids and a house to prove it.

If there was anything he knew, it was that women liked power and money over everything else, and he had both of those. Sure, it might not be enough to keep someone happy forever, but it was enough to at least hook someone. Especially a person like Missy, who clearly needed someone to take care of her.

~~~

Missy was quiet. She wanted to have a response, but she was thinking about Jay. When she got home, she'd be alone in her big quiet apartment, with no one to talk to about her day, no one to tell about creepy Mr. Richards, no one to hold her and tell her he loved her; no one. She'd dreaded going home every day since the break up.

Sure, Missy had friends, really good friends at that, but they weren't Jay and they were sick of hearing about him.

Mr. Richards could see that her young mind was working feverishly. "You okay, Missy?"

Missy snapped back to reality. "Oh, yeah, I'm fine. Just tired, and I have a lot of things to do before tomorrow."

"Well, don't worry too much about being there on time tomorrow. I'll tell Mrs. Richards that you were at the house late and had some things you had to do. She'll understand."

"Thanks Mr. Richards," Missy said. She really had nothing pressing to do. All this meant was that she was going to be able to drink for longer tonight, or sleep in; either of the two.

The rest of the ride was long and excruciating. Mr. Richards kept asking questions about Missy and her personal life. She didn't want to talk, but needed to keep conversation flowing. She could feel his bulging eyes on her.

Mr. Richards had the weirdest eyes; it was like as he got fatter his eyes did too, and they were fixed on her. Missy couldn't be positive, but it definitely seemed like that was the case. She answered questions about school, her hopes and dreams, the things she wanted for herself, but every answer was hollow and empty.

Missy felt like none of it mattered if Jay wasn't there. He had never responded to any of the letters she sent and it broke her heart even more. She'd written him every week in that first year after they broke up, then she stopped when he never said anything back. She'd written a few more a couple of months back, but still no response. Jay wasn't the kind of guy to blow her off and she didn't understand his lack of response. She even thought he had maybe moved, but when she walked by his apartment one day she saw him through the window. And since none of them had been returned, he'd either read them all or thrown them away; she wasn't sure which was worse.

Missy wasn't stalking Jay, she just happened to take that route home that day, or at least that's what she told herself. Never mind that it was about 15 minutes out of the way.

~~~

Milton knew all about Jay and the unanswered letters. He was the reason they'd never reached Jay. Working at a post office for a few months, Milton had learned a few useful things. One of them was that love letters were never a good thing. Someone was always more invested emotionally than the other and the letters only made things harder. One party got sadder and the other felt guilty. Because of this, he collected all the love letters that came his way. Like an Angel of Death to relationships.

This is how he found out about Missy in the first place. Her letters to Jay were beautiful, and quite honestly belonged in a book of poems, but Milton knew Jay wouldn't appreciate them the way that they deserved. This is why Milton kept the letters. Through them, he got to know Missy, and he developed quite an affinity for this heartbroken girl and her painstakingly crafted notes to the love of her short life. The fact that Jay, whoever he was, had deserted Missy only convinced Milton more that Jay was undeserving of Missy's love. She was so full of life, so full of emotion, that it just wasn't fair for Jay to take advantage of it. She deserved the attention of someone like Milton, someone who would cherish her, and that's exactly what he did.

Sure, he had to wait awhile to follow Missy, since the letters started a year and a half ago, but that's why he enjoyed following her so much, despite how sad and lonely she was. Milton found her fascinating.

Finally, Mr. Richards pulled up to Missy's apartment. Milton slid into a parking spot on the street behind them.

~~~

Missy couldn't wait to get out of the car and run up to her apartment. As she gathered her things, she hastily turned to Mr. Richards to thank him. It was a quick 'thank you' done in passing, nothing sincere about it. As she did it, he caught her hand and held it for a few seconds. She had a look of horror on her face, thinking "What is he going to do?!"

~~~

Mr. Richards mistook Missy's horror for surprise and excitement, which aroused him. He hadn't meant to grab her hand, it was almost a reflex. He'd been thinking about how he was going to make his move the whole ride home. Wasted thoughts because the action had happened without him thinking.

But he was hoping that she would reciprocate the action, clutching back at his hand. That didn't happen though, and Mr. Richards could tell immediately that he'd made the wrong decision.

Trying to make it less awkward, Mr. Richards loosened his grip and started patting Missy's hand instead, saying, "Give it time. You'll love him less and less every day."

~~~

The moment before he let her go was silent and eternal. "See you tomorrow Missy. Sweet dreams," he smiled at her.

She was relieved beyond words that he hadn't tried anything further. She simply responded, "Uh huh, thanks," and fumbled with opening the car door, then ran as fast as she could up her apartment stairs. She pressed the wrong code to get in several times before she got it, and slipped through the door.

Mr. Richards' eyes burned into her back the whole way, as he waited in his car until the light in her apartment turned on.

Missy looked out her window and saw his car still there. He waved at her and drove away. Her stomach dropped and she quickly scanned the street, wondering if there was anyone else watching her.

Drinking didn't even appeal to Missy right now, she

was too freaked out. She just ate a brownie, turned off her lights and went to sleep.

~~~

Milton's car was nearly invisible; it looked just like any other car on any other block; hidden from sight to the sweeping eye. Throughout his life he'd found that he was the man you had seen a million times, but had never taken note of, despite the fact that he was a real person.

When Missy's room was dark, Milton started his drive home, an hour away.

Milton didn't mind the long drive home. It gave him time to think. He could sort out the events he had observed that day and get ready for the next one. While there were many things in his past he could dwell on and obsess over, he chose to be completely consumed by the thoughts of his subject, whoever he or she may be.

He'd started down this path at a very young age. The first person Milton stalked was his own mother. She just assumed it was boyish curiosity, until she started finding him in odd places, like her dirty clothes hamper, peeking out from under the lid. When she uncovered him, he was holding a little notepad that was full of sketches of her. They were remedial, but enough to let her know that her son needed some boundaries. No one needed to see crayon drawings of her boobs.

Milton's mother did everything in her power to teach him that watching people when they didn't know it was not okay, but it just never took. He'd ask her what the difference was between watching people on TV and in real life? She'd tell him that it just was different, that's all. This never made sense to him and he continued following her around, taking notes about her.

When Milton was six, his father died. He had been an advertising executive and left Milton and his mother with more money than they knew what to do with. This meant that they had a huge house and endless resources at their disposal. Because of this, Milton's mother worried about her son going to a public school. She was paranoid about him being kidnapped and held for ransom, so she home-schooled him instead.

A tutor came to live with them full-time, but that didn't last long.

The first tutor, Mrs. MacIntosh, quit when she found Milton hiding in her tub behind the shower curtain. He was watching her as she went to the bathroom. She wouldn't even have noticed him, but she heard some scratching noises from behind the curtain; the sound of pencil scratching paper. Mrs. MacIntosh pulled back the curtain and saw little Milton sitting there inside the shower sketching her on the toilet. She screamed and hastily pulled up her panties, getting piss all over the floor.

Milton was terribly embarrassed, but he just stayed right there writing away. He wanted to observe Mrs. MacIntosh's reaction and figure out why she had gotten so scared. The fact that he remained in the tub, staring at her, seemed to horrify Mrs. MacIntosh even more, which confused Milton because he was just a little boy. She hurriedly packed her things and left the house. On the way out, she ran into Milton's mother who asked where she was going. Mrs. MacIntosh simply said that she would not spend anymore time educating a future serial killer.

She didn't want to admit it, but Milton's mother had a pretty good idea about what had just happened. When she found Milton, he was sitting on his bed, looking like a sad puppy whose squeak toy just broke. His mother looked at him, cupping his chin in her hand. Then with one quick motion, she slapped him hard on the face. Milton's eyes welled with tears, as if the emotional pain of what just happened hurt more than the physical. His mother stared him in the eye, then closed his door and locked it from the outside.

With her husband gone, Mother didn't know what to do. She couldn't have her son creeping around the house, scaring everybody, but what other options did she have? He couldn't stay locked up forever, and kids were supposed to be curios, weren't they? After thinking for an hour or two, she went back up to her son's room and unlocked the door. He was sitting on the edge of his bed, staring at the wall, obviously deep in thought. She walked over to Milton, and knelt in front of him so they were eye-to-eye.

"Sweetie, do you know why I hit you?" she asked.

He nodded his head yes.

Mother looked surprised. "Well then tell me."

Milton sat up. He spoke slowly, "I'm not supposed to watch people."

"Right. So why were you watching Mrs. MacIntosh?"

"I just wanted to know what she was doing. I like knowing what people are doing. I like watching them and writing it down."

Milton's mother didn't know how to respond. It sounded innocent enough, and she assumed it could just be a phase, but the thought lingered in her head, what if it isn't; what if this obsession with stalking people becomes something more. She couldn't live with herself if he hurt someone, nor could she live with the thought of someone hiding in every nook and cranny watching her every move. The thought alone began to drive her mad.

As the years went on, Milton went through four more tutors and dozens of nannies. He was an well-behaved child and didn't need a nanny, but his mother knew if there were more people around, there was less of a chance that Milton would be watching her. Their house was so big that she never knew where he was at any given time, but she assumed he wasn't near her. As the years went by and the house staff quit, Milton's mother began to loathe her own son.

~~~

One sunny day, Milton's mother was sunbathing on the roof. She'd had her husband build a small balcony up there because it was the one place where she could tan in the nude and no one would see. She also claimed you got a better tan when you were closer to the sun.

Well, on this particular day, Milton's mother was in the nude, as usual, only the pool boy had accompanied her onto the roof this time. Milton had already hidden himself in a bush near the edge, which scared him so he made sure not to look down. Luckily, he was on the one side that was hedged so nothing was visible from the street.

Milton was still situation himself in the shrub when he saw the pool boy take off his clothes and get on top of his naked mother. She started yelling. Milton didn't know what to do. He wanted to stay hidden and take notes, but he had to help his mother!

In an instant, Milton charged the pool boy. He burst through the bushes aiming right for the pantsless man. There was no stopping him. With all the force of an 11-year-old boy, he ran right into his mother's lover, who stumbled, staggered and fell off the roof of the house, screaming louder than his mother had been.

Most people will recall an event like that saying that it happened so fast, but not for Milton or his mother. For them, it all happened in excruciatingly slow motion. The man fell four stories, and when he hit the ground, Milton thought it looked like when he dropped water balloons off the roof. He smiled, because he didn't understand death yet, and thought the man looked funny falling. Milton's mother, horrified, just stared at her smiling son. She was dumbstruck, and suddenly felt an urge to throw Milton off the roof too, to teach him a lesson.

She walked over to her son, and grabbed him hard by the shoulders. His smile quickly faded and he now wore the look of fear and concern. He tried to cry, but no tears came. His mother walked him to the very edge of the roof. The only thing that kept him from falling was his resistance against her forceful hands.

They stood there for a few seconds, fighting gravity and desire, until his mother finally let Milton go. She pulled him into her arms, sobbing. Milton had no emotion other than confusion. He hadn't processed all of what had just happened, because he just didn't understand it. In a matter of seconds he'd seen his mother being defiled, pushed her attacker and almost been shoved by the woman he wanted to save.

Milton's mother took him downstairs and locked him in his room again. He sat there for what seemed like hours. He could see police cars outside his window and saw an ambulance. They were putting something inside that was in a black bag. Milton thought it was the pool boy because of the shape and size, and he wondered how the man could breathe in there. When the ambulance left, a different white van drove up. He hadn't seen that kind of van before and wondered what it was. Two men dressed in white got out and were led into the house.

Milton could hear voices below him, but didn't know what they were saying. He laid back down on his bed and stared at the ceiling. It was killing him that he wasn't down there watching what was going on. More than anything he was upset that he was missing out on the action. There was no one down there to write everything down. How would anyone remember those moments? Next thing he knew, he was banging on his own door, screaming and crying "Let me out! Somebody! Anybody! Mother! Let me out!!" He was crying so hard that snot and drool ran down his face as he struggled to breathe. By the time the two men in white got the the room with his mother, Milton looked like a caged, wild animal.

All Milton wanted was to see what was going on, but no one would listen. They began to put a white jacket on him. He struggled, but his mother bent down and looked him in the eye. She said, "Sweetie, these men are friends of mine. They're taking you on a vacation. This is a magic jacket they're putting on you so don't struggle, just let them put it on. Where you're going, I won't be there. Every time you wear this jacket, think of me holding you. It's like you're wearing one of Mother's big, warm hugs. Okay sweetie?"

Milton nodded, sniffling and crying. He looked like a brave boy.

"Be good for these men Milton, and remember, every time you have that jacket on, you're getting a big hug from me."

Milton tried to be a big boy, but as they walked him away from the house, he looked back and saw his mother standing in the doorway. He began screaming and crying, "Mother!" He realized in that moment that they were taking him away from the only person he loved, and without her, he had no one to follow. He didn't know where he was going, or if there was anyone there as interesting as his mother. He needed her. He needed to watch her, to know what she was doing at all times. In this new place, he was going to be alone, and that was more than he could bear.

The two men put him in the white truck. Before they strapped him to the bed inside, he caught a glimpse of his mother. She was hugging herself, in the same position the jacket had his arms in. As they were about to leave, she smiled and blew Milton a kiss just before the doors of the truck slammed shut. That was the last time Milton ever saw his mother.

~~~

By the time he got out of the mental facility, Milton was 18-years-old. He was deemed safe to be released into society. However, when he returned to his home, he found it in good shape but empty. The people from the hospital had taken him home; apparently the arrangements had all been made by someone, but Milton didn't know who.

As he walked through the front door, memories slowly started coming back to Milton. Mostly the memory of the last time that he saw his mother. After seven years, he was curious about how she looked; if age had gotten the best of her. As he walked through those front doors, all Milton wanted was to see her. Oddly, he never resented the fact that she never came to see him in the hospital. He wouldn't have gone either if he didn't have to.

"Mother!" he yelled out, excited to see her smile.

Milton started running through the house, to all of Mother's favorite rooms, hoping to see her. She wasn't in her bedroom, or the den, or on the roof. When he entered the dining room though, there was a note on the table next to a vase of fresh flowers. Mother loved fresh flowers. The note read "Milton, Welcome home. Your mother passed away last night in the hospital. Apologies I couldn't be there to tell you in person, but I had to take care of her affairs. She left the home and all of her money to you. I'll be by in the morning to discuss the details of the exact amount. Sincere sympathies, Philip J. Robinson, Esq. Attorney at Law"

It took reading the note several times for the news to sink in. Milton had known that Mother wasn't well, and that she was in the hospital a few times to treat her breast cancer, but she'd told him she was fine in their phone calls. Hadn't she?

The realization was slowly creeping over Milton, that he hadn't talked to his mother in months. She was on her death bed this whole time, and she'd never called him. Feeling alone, he wondered if he was the one who truly killed Mother.

Milton looked around. Everything was just as he remembered it, except for his mother's absence. Nothing would be the same now that she was gone. He had spent the last seven years of his life enduring electro-shock therapy and taking high doses of medication to keep him compliant. Some of the things Milton went through were so inhumane that he vowed never to speak of them again. Every tactic, experimental or otherwise had been utilized to get him to realize that stalking people was wrong. He hated how they talked about it, like it was a creepy thing.

To Milton, it was like watching television. He reasoned that most TV shows are just an audience looking in on other people's lives, watching them. How was what he was doing any different? He genuinely wanted to know what people were doing; he wanted to watch them. He needed to watch them. Milton had convinced the people at the psych ward that he was cured, but he knew he wasn't. He just missed freedom.

Now that the object of his fixation was gone, Milton had no idea what to do. He couldn't stop following people. That was not an option. He needed to find someone else. There had to be another person to fill his insatiable need to watch the true drama of life unfold, to watch real action. But how would he find someone? He lived in a house on a hill with no one around him for acres.

Milton decided that the only way to fill his need was to leave and go to the city. There he would find people of all sorts to choose from. He could find the perfect person that looked and acted just like Mother did.

~~~

The next day, Milton didn't wait for the lawyer Phillip Esquire, or whoever, to get there. He started up his mother's car, which he had never officially learned to drive, and attempted to make his way into the city, an hour away. At first he struggled, but then driving came naturally to him, after about an hour of practice. He navigated into the city and found a big park.

Milton's clothes were very old, because they were his father's. When he arrived home, there were none his own size, so he stood out in the crowd, which was counterproductive to his purposes. As soon as he realized this, he sought out the nearest store. After trying on several outfits, he decided on a white shirt and khaki pants, something simple, that would blend in. What he hadn't counted on was not having any money on him to pay for the clothes.

Realizing he'd made a crucial mistake, Milton left and angrily went home for his meeting with the lawyer. He couldn't imagine his mother having spent all of the money Father left them; certainly she loved him more than that. But then again, she did send him away without so much as a visit around the holidays.

The drive home seemed to take longer than before, but the clock showed that it had been just under an hour. When Milton opened the door, the lawyer was waiting at the table. He took one look at Milton, still in his father's clothes, and knew he was in for a crazy afternoon. Milton shook his hand and sat down at the table. The lawyer began explaining the terms of the will.

Milton was pleased to know he was left with millions of dollars. What he was not pleased to learn was that it was contingent upon him never stalking another person in his life. If he was caught doing so, the money was to be given to charity immediately and he was to be banned from the premises. Even in death, his mother had been a vindictive woman. She was depriving him of the one thing that brought him joy; "How could she not see that?" Milton wondered, even though deep down he knew that she understood it too well.

Finally agreeing to the terms, Milton signed all of the necessary paperwork, and the lawyer left. Milton decided to stay in that night. If he was to keep his money, he had to be more cautious about his activities in the city so that he was never caught stalking. Thus started a long journey for Milton.

~~~

When Milton was left his mother's house the next day, he didn't know what to do. He had to find someone to watch, anyone, someone who looked like Mother preferably. This is when he found Caitlin. She was his first.

Milton saw Caitlin at the post office, standing in line. He maneuvered his way so that he was behind her and could hear what she was saying to the cashier. She was prattling on about how her employer made her come to the post office at least twice a day (if not more), how long the lines were, and on and on.

Oddly, Milton was very interested in this, but it was

mostly because she looked and sounded so much like his mother; the resemblance was uncanny.

When Milton got up to the front to buy a book of stamps, he noticed a sign stating that they were hiring. Working at a post office was exactly what he needed to fill his time. It would keep him busy, he'd get to see plenty of people, *and* it was in the city. "Perfect," he thought to himself.

"What position are you hiring for?" Milton asked the short, odd looking man at the desk, who happened to also be eerily jolly. His disposition in no way matched his physical appearance.

"Well, this very position right here, young sir. I'm retiring!" he had a stupid, smug look on his face.

Milton applied for the job right there and then, leaving out his past in the mental health facility. The next day he received a call that he needed to come in for an interview. During the drive to the city, Milton couldn't help but think about Caitlin. He hoped beyond all hope that she would be on one of her many post office runs when he got there for the interview. Sure enough, she was! Milton was so happy at the sight of her that he was positive he'd aced his interview..

Thus started the stalking of Caitlin.

~~~

Every time Caitlin came into the post office, Milton would chat with her, and help her get things done faster. In time, she knew to just walk up to his window and he'd always take her next. This was both good and bad since she was thrilled to get out of there quickly, but he was sad to see her leave. And it wasn't long until he took note of her employer's address.

One day after work, on a day when Milton got off unusually early because of a miscommunication about shifts, he went by the employer's building, which was boldly written on all of the packages Missy dropped off to ship. It was in the wealthy part of town; a place he felt very comfortable in. The building itself looked more like a little townhouse than an office building, but Milton knew sometimes people worked out of their homes.

Milton drove by the place a few times, slowing down more each time. Then, finally, he stopped, parked, and waited outside. It was getting dark and he wasn't entirely sure that Caitlin was still inside, but he had a feeling she was. It was the same feeling he got when he knew she walked into the post office before he even saw her.

Finally Caitlin came out of the house. Milton ducked down in his seat and looked for his notebook. He slid it out from his pocket and began to write some notes down in it:

Wearing simple black shirt and jeans with matching sneakers. Gets into a black two-door Honda Civic and drives away quickly.

When Caitlin turned on her lights, Milton didn't turn on his, he just quietly followed her out of that wealthy neighborhood. Following Caitlin was when he learned the ability to drive without any headlights on.

That night Milton followed Caitlin all the way to her apartment. Now that he knew where she lived, he could do some serious stalking, like finding her exact apartment and try to get inside while she was out.

Yes, Caitlin was Milton's first post-mental hospital victim.

Over the next few months, Milton found out everything that there was to know about this girl. He broke into her house, read her diaries, and filled up his own journal about her. He became completely obsessed. On his work breaks, he would reread what he had previously written down about Caitlin.

Finally, the time came where Caitlin's journal was

filled, and Milton had to move on. This was not easy for him because he knew that he'd never see her again. He had to find a special way of saying goodbye, some way that she'd remember him as much he'd remember her. Since he knew everything about her, he decided on simply giving her a flower, her favorite.

That night when Caitlin got home, she found a stargazer lily outside of her apartment door with a note attached to it. The note read: "It's been lovely getting to know you these last months, following you from afar. I'll never forget the time we spent together, but I must move on."

Caitlin heard a noise down the hall and it startled her. She quickly looked and saw a man's shadow rounding the corner, moving away from her. The message and flower, coupled with the noise had scared her, but she didn't know what to do, so she went inside and put the lily in a vase with water. After all, she couldn't just let it die.

~~~

Milton was so sad to leave Caitlin that he couldn't bring himself to drive away. He hurried out of the apartment building and got a place where he could watch her. He stared at Caitlin through her window as she delicately placed her flower in vase. She lovingly spruced it up and made it look beautiful, just like her.

He stood there watching her, but it was different this time. It was like a film student who finally got to watch a movie without taking notes on it, or a cook who just got to enjoy a meal. After a while though, as everyone does with an empty-headed beautiful woman, Milton got bored. He looked down at the journal in his hand. It was full, but he felt empty. He knew he had to find someone else, and fast. He needed something to do; someone to watch.

Speeding home, all Milton could think about was this void. He kept looking to the journal on his passenger seat, knowing he could never go back to Caitlin again. Like when you have a drunken fight with a lover; words are thrown and you know you can never be together again.

The drive seemed long and quiet, and Milton yearned for this emptiness to be filled, by anything. He realized this was harder than he had anticipated, so he got off the freeway in a hurry, the very next exit. He was right by the not-so-great part of town, and he knew right where to go.

While he was in the mental hospital, Milton had heard about strip clubs and strippers from the old, creepy men. They talked about ass and titties all day long, each claiming he'd seen some better than the next guy had. Milton had first seen a naked woman when he was spying on his mom, but he'd never thought of her in *that* way. He just liked observing her parts, the way they were shaped, how they moved as she walked around.

It was all very scientific.

So, Milton found himself at the Star Light Lounge, sitting right in the front, watching the woman on the stage dance. She swayed and ground herself into the pole, climbing up and sliding down to the rhythm.

Milton wished he had a journal on his person so he could notate the fullness of her breasts and how, oddly enough, they weren't bouncy. Implants, he mentally noted. He was so frightened that he'd forget these important details by the time he got a new journal. Then, a girl tapped him on the shoulder from behind his left shoulder. Startled, he jumped and turned around.

"Didn't mean to scare you mister. Just wanted to know if you wanted a dance."

The woman smiled at him sweetly, as she put her hands on his shoulders and straddled his legs. Milton simply nodded, as he took in what she looked like. Her hair was long and black, and Milton was fairly sure that it was a wig. She had too much glitter on her eyes, but looking closer, he decided it was to hide her true age, which wasn't young. Her body was okay, but that wasn't why he was here anyway.

Not wanting to stand out, Milton nodded without smiling, and motioned for her to start. "Don't you want to go to the back where it's more private?" she asked.

Milton thought about this briefly. He spent most of his life trying not to be noticed, and now he was in a place where everyone tried not to acknowledge each other. It was the perfect chance to watch, and it was expected of him. "No, right here is just fine," he responded.

She began dancing, hovering over him, shaking her slightly sagging butt in his face. Then she turned so he could see her full bosom. He was rapidly taking mental notes, struggling to not forget a single moment of this, should this stripper be the one he decided to follow. He couldn't forget, he *needed* to remember.

Then he saw *her* from across the room: a gorgeous red head who was vigorously grinding on a 60-something balding man with had a stupid grin on his face. Milton's first thought was that someone should slap the smile off him (Milton considered all grins to be stupid, because they are), and rescue her; take her away from this awful place so he could study her.

Then it hit him. She would be his next. He would forget Caitlin once and for all, and move on to Ginger (that's what he mentally named the redhead until he found out her real name).

Milton abruptly stood up in between the ample breasts of the stripper who was still dancing on him. She yelled, acting offended, then he threw a $50 bill at her and she went silent. She waved off the approaching bouncer, and wedged the bill in her thong straps.

After the dance ended, Milton turned and watched as Ginger danced, taking note of what she was wearing, her height, her approximate weight, anything he could gather. But not having a journal there with him began to weigh on Milton, because he could forget so many details. He got up and quickly left the strip club.

Milton drove off, speeding towards his house. He had found Ginger, his next subject, and he couldn't stop thinking about her. By the time he got to his home, he was already obsessed.

Milton unceremoniously threw out Caitlin, symbolically, by tossing the journal in a corner to be organized and cataloged later. There was no time right now. He quickly found another empty journal lying around his house, opened it up and began writing down everything regarding Ginger that he could remember.

Grinds against old men and seems to like it. The older men pay her for "lap dances." Seems to enjoy the attention and smiles throughout. She has a fantastic head of full, long red hair. She looks like Ariel, if Ariel had double D breasts and wide-set hips.

Milton wrote every remaining memory he had of Ginger, which lasted half a page. He sat there, in the quiet, in the dark of that mansion, and decided he needed to go back and see this stripper.

So, Milton got back in his car and drove with his journal in-hand. When he made it back into the club, he looked around, obviously searching for something, or someone. Either way he looked out of place. Like a googly eyed prepubescent boy. Finally, Milton saw her.

Ginger was on the stage, where the other dancers had been before. She was grinding on that same pole, rubbing her barely-clothed body all over it. Milton had to suppress his desire to vomit at the thought about the myriad of diseases and germs that were festering on that big, long, shiny pole.

Milton sat down to watch her perform, but the song had come to an end. He caught her eye and waved her over. She smiled sweetly, which he noted before she got there, and led him away to a back room. Now that he'd found his next subject, there was no need to stay out with everyone else.

Once they were alone, with the music blaring, he noted the rhythm she danced in. Slightly off, almost as if she was dancing to her own beat. He mentally noted:
* Find out if she is a natural red head.

That was very important information. So, Ginger continued dancing, and Milton continued observing, unsmiling. Watching the curves of her body and how the light hit them, how she moved with the light.

Milton kept watching her movements, observing rather than participating and taking them in, so when the song ended and she asked for her money it took him a minute to remember that she had been dancing *for* him. He quickly reached in his pocket and handed her a few large bills.

~~~

Ginger noticed that this John wasn't smiling and was a bit creeped out by his eyes, boring into her, as though he were studying her. She asked herself, "What kind of a weirdo can just sit there, like he's analyzing my body? As if I need anymore scrutiny." At the end of the song, Ginger quickly asked for her money in an attempt to get the hell out of there.

While Ginger thought this was the oddest man she'd ever seen, she needed money, and he was tipping really well. So, she went ahead and asked if he wanted another dance. In his odd, expressionless, monotone voice he responded, "Yes. That would be good." So she danced.

Ginger ended up dancing for the little man all night and walked away with a wad of cash in her hand. Later on, as she was getting ready to leave and head home, she had a weird feeling, like she was being watched. She just chalked it up to being weirded out by that odd dude all night, and kept seeing his emotionless face in her mind.

Paul, the bouncer, was standing by the door and Ginger asked him to walk her to her car. He asked if someone had been bothering her tonight. She said no, but just that she'd feel safer with a big strong man next to her.

~~~

Happily, but still watchful, Paul walked through the parking lot with her, surveying the area for anything that was out of place. Ginger was a tough girl, and she rarely asked for an escort to her car, so he had a feeling something was up. He looked at all the cars in the parking lot, which wasn't very many. He zeroed in on a sedan in the corner; it looked like a man was sitting inside the driver's seat staring at them. Paul shined his light in the direction of the car, but no dice, the car was empty.

After he made sure that Ginger had safely arrived at, and started her car, Paul began to walk back towards the club. He glanced around the parking lot again. Once Ginger had pulled out of the lot, the sedan he thought was empty, suddenly started, but the lights weren't on. The car pulled out of the parking lot, lightless, and it was still impossible to see the driver. Paul thought about calling Ginger, but thought, it's probably just a drunk guy. No sense in alarming her.

~~~

While she was driving, Ginger still couldn't shake this weird feeling that she was being watched. There weren't many cars on the street, but enough to make it hard to tell if someone was following you. She was sure that no one was, that she was still just unnerved by that man, but she still couldn't shake it.

Ginger was not the type of woman to overreact. She grew up with brothers and they'd taught her how to protect herself, how to evade any possible bad situations. Also, she was studying criminology at the local city college, so she decided to employ the evasive techniques they taught them. Then she heard a loud honk and screeching of tires behind her.

~~~

Milton was using this as an opportunity to test his driving-without-headlights skills. He was getting much better at it, and actually began enjoying it. It was like he was invisible, gliding along the roads, and no one could see him. He felt impenetrable, like a secret agent or something, who was sent to observe this large-bosomed redhead. The hardest part of driving with no lights, he found, was getting other cars to avoid you. Late at night, all drivers were tired, and all they wanted to do was get home, not look out for secret agents driving without their headlights.

So, as lightless Milton was following Ginger, he had a run-in and narrowly escaped a crash when he didn't notice her stopping. He'd gone deep in thought, daydreaming about where Ginger lived and what her home looked like. Coming to a stop sign, he halted his car, as Ginger had done with hers, then continued across the intersection. A car coming the opposite way, however, had already decided that he was going to run through the stop sign since he saw no cars there anyway.

~~~

The unidentified driver was speeding down the road, swerving for fun, then, as he got closer, he realized there was a car without its lights on in the intersection. The driver of the speeding car honked and slammed on his breaks, trying to avoid the horrible, oblivious dumbass who forgotten to turn his lights on.

Milton was startled by the honking. He didn't know where it was coming from, then he saw the headlights. He quickly slammed his foot on the gas, his car jumping forward and taking off, towards Ginger's vehicle. Luckily she was far enough ahead that he wouldn't come close to hitting her, but not so far that she wouldn't hear the honking.

The near-accident should have made him scared for his life, but Milton was more scared of being found out. He had chosen his next subject and he couldn't afford to be found out. Luckily she hadn't made any indication of noticing him.

~~~

Ginger heard the ruckus and looked in her rear view mirror. As she did, she saw a car behind her turn on its lights. She hadn't noticed the car before, but that was probably because it was dark, she rationalized. "How could anyone forget to turn their headlights on," she wondered to herself. But, the important thing was now they were on and whoever that driver was wouldn't endanger anyone else.

As she drove, Ginger noticed the car with the headlights was still following her. She lived in an area where there were lots of other people, so it was entirely possible that he just happened to live in the same place as her, but she still couldn't shake that weird feeling she had. She decided to take a few extra minutes and drive around the block, checking to see if she indeed was being followed. She drove down her street first, surveying the parking situation, which looked horrible. She'd probably end up having to drive around the block anyway.

Then, Ginger turned onto another street. The car with the headlights did the same. "Maybe he's looking for parking too," she thought, trying the keep her heart rate normal. More than the idea of someone following her, she was scared of the idea about how to handle the situation. Ginger did not like confrontation, but she liked being followed even less. If this creep caught up to her though, she'd let him have it. She turned another corner, her third left.

~~~

Milton realized what was happening, or what he thought was happening. Ginger was leading him around, seeing if his car was following hers. If only he hadn't had to turn the damn headlights on. There were lots of people that lived in the area, so he decided to head her off and act like he was looking for parking.

She finally got back to her street, and as she slowly turned onto it, Ginger realized the car was still following her. She began to slow her vehicle, and eventually brought the car to a stop, and double parked it. With pepper spray in hand, the stripper began to get out of the car to go confront whoever this was. She'd need to see him to tell the police what he looked like anyways.

~~~

Milton could see what was about to happen and enacted his plan – there was a plan for every situation. He turned on his blinker and went around Ginger's car, spotting a car up ahead who was pulling out of a parking spot. He quickly zoomed past Ginger, who was already out of her car and heading for him. Milton got to the spot just as someone was pulling out.

"That was too close for comfort," he thought to himself, acting as though he was getting his things together to go into his non-existent apartment.

Remembering that Ginger was heading for his car, Milton kept an eye on his rear view mirror, until she finally went back inside her own vehicle.

~~~

Getting back into her car, Ginger felt silly and defeated. She looked around to see if anyone had seen what she had been about to do. No. Phew. She got back in her car and resumed her search for a parking place, furious that she'd let this stranger get the best of her and make her lose her chance to park close to home. She eventually found a spot.

Carefully hidden in his car, Milton waited for Ginger to come back around. He had a strong feeling that she lived on this street and he had to find out where. He had to watch her walk into a building so that he knew what he was dealing with and could strategize the best way to watch her without being seen.

This particular street had a lot of trees. A person could easily hide in these trees and look into all the windows. This shouldn't be too hard at all.

~~~

Ginger got home, and cautiously looked around her apartment. She knew everything was fine and normal, but she still felt the need to check in every little space. She looked in her closet, under her bed, behind the shower curtain, and as she expected, nothing. Everything was just as it should have been. But she couldn't shake the feeling that she was being watched. She knew it.

As it turned out, she was right, but she wouldn't know it for weeks.

~~~

Milton observed the building Ginger disappeared into, taking note of which light flickered to life around the time she walked in. He saw a window brighten and walked around to that side of the house. It was a window on the second floor, but it faced the street, which was lucky for him. Milton climbed a tree on the same side of the street as the building. It was a tall tree with strong branches and lots of foliage, which was another stroke of luck. From here, he could see everything, while still staying hidden from sight.

Milton watched Ginger as she moved around her apartment. It was small, but clean, almost to the point of looking sterile. The décor was sparse, with the exception of a few photographs on the walls and one painting of the Eiffel Tower. It was just a studio with a stove and refrigerator taking up the entirety of the kitchen space. Milton watched as Ginger went to the fridge and pulled out an apple. She washed it and shined it with a dishtowel before taking a big bite. As she ate, she undressed, piece by piece. He watched her, even though he'd seen the majority of her body over the last few hours. He watched as she took off everything and laid it all in the middle of the floor. She walked naked through a doorway which he assumed led to the bathroom, though he couldn't tell from his angle. He sat there patiently waiting for her to emerge.

~~~

Even as she showered, Ginger felt uneasy. She'd checked everything and the apartment seemed fine. Nothing was under her bed, there wasn't a person hiding in her shower, and other than that, there was nowhere a human being could even fit. There was no explanation for why she still had this urging inside her; a feeling that she needed to look around a little more.

Ginger wasn't a girl who scared easily either. She was very aware, very perceptive, and always had a clear head, but she just knew something wasn't right.

After finishing her shower, she walked out into her room, looking for some nightclothes to put on. It was then that she realized her window was open. This wasn't unusual because it was always open since there was no way anyone could see in. She was on the second floor, and it was a high second floor. One of those second floors where the lobby of the building was considered a lobby and not a first floor, so really, she was on the third floor. The only thing she could see out of the window, when she stood in the middle of her room, was a tree. A big, giant tree that had grown on the street for generations, since long before she'd moved there. She looked at the tree, thinking maybe there was something in *there* that was making her uneasy.

Ginger stared hard at the tree, slowly walking towards her window. As she looked, she began to see the shape of something, something that she thought might have been a person crouched in the branches. "That's crazy," she thought to herself, "but crazy enough to be true." She kept staring at the tree in the dark, her eyes trying desperately to make a shape out of any of the shadows. She thought she saw something move, but after staring at the branches for a few minutes, she decided her eyes were playing tricks on her and shut the curtains, and the window.

~~~

The whole time Ginger had been peering out, Milton had been holding his breath. She was staring right at him, searching, and he was sure his cover was blown. Her eyes were fixed right on him, like a laser beam, but it was as if he was invisible. She couldn't see him, somehow. Just then, his foot slipped, just a little, but it was enough for her to zero in on him even more. Her eyes darted around, looking for whatever it was that she thought she had seen. Then, suddenly, she slammed her window shut and drew the curtains.

This was Milton's cue to leave. He'd see nothing more of Ginger tonight, but he was determined to be back, early in the morning, and study her habits even more. He'd started a new journal and he had to find out all that he could about this woman by following her around. The walk back to his car seemed to take forever, but he got there, started the ignition, and made sure to turn on his headlights before beginning the long drive home.

To pass the time, Milton kept thinking about how lucky he had been not to get caught, and that he needed a better strategy for following this stripper. The tree had been a risky choice. He wasn't sure how she'd seen him in there, or why she hadn't done anything about it, but he knew he needed a better plan. The next time he'd bring some war paint, like the kind they use in the military. This way his face wouldn't be seen at all. He'd wear all black, brown and green clothes too, but not camo because it wouldn't match that particular tree.

One thing was clear: Milton needed to go shopping.

As soon as he walked in the front door, Milton saw

the journal he'd carelessly flung in the corner; all his observations about Caitlin. He'd thrown her out like an old rag. A proper parting of ways was needed, he decided. So he planned a dinner for them, just him and the journal. He called his favorite restaurant, but it was closed. His special dinner would have to wait until the next day, because Milton had no idea how to cook anything besides breakfast. Setting the journal on the kitchen table, he headed upstairs to go to bed.

~~~

The next morning, Milton woke up at 5am. He didn't know what Ginger's plans were for the day, but he knew that he didn't want to miss any part of them. He had to get there early. As he went downstairs he passed Caitlin's journal on the table. He looked at it, guiltily, as if it knew that he was cheating on her. He wasn't, but it was true that he hadn't properly tended to Caitlin yet; that is to say, they hadn't quite broken up.

There was no way Milton could leave with this book giving him the evil eye, like it knew where he was going. He had to end this now, so he started to make some eggs. He thought bacon and orange juice would have been nice as well, but he had neither, so he just made sure that the eggs he made were very delicious.

He placed them on a plate and poured himself a glass

of water. Then he sat opposite the journal, which he had propped up using an empty cereal bowl. He explained himself:

"This is not about you, you've been great, this is about me. I've spent enough time with you to know that I don't want to spend anymore. I need to move on. In secret, when no one can see you, that's when you find out who you really are. And after watching you for awhile now, I know you really are a great person. Really. But I just don't want to spend time with you anymore. I've found someone else. I've moved on. We both knew this wasn't forever, that it had to end, and that time has come. I'll never forget you Caitlin."

Then Milton finished his eggs, in an awkward silence between him and the scorned journal. He ate his breakfast slowly, not in a hurry to get out of there, savoring them as much as he was his last official moments with Caitlin.

As soon as he finished, he took the journal and put it on the shelf, next to his other books and journals of notable famous people. He put it there as if it belonged with the thoughts of those far greater than him. While he put the book on the shelf, he promised himself that never again would he begin a new journal before ending the old one, completely. An air of sadness and guilt swept over him. But as soon as the journal was placed on the shelf, the feeling quickly subsided and the only thing he could think about was Ginger. He had to get to Ginger, before she woke up.

She was his world now.

~~~

Ginger worked late, but she also had school early. She worked very hard to make sure that her private life stayed private, which is why she chose to work and go to school in places that were over an hour away from each other. Her school was a junior college, just until she could get the money to move and go to a real university.

Her parents had died when she was very young, and the last words Ginger's mom said to her were, "Make sure you go to college." So, she did. Lacey, Ginger's mom, had been an uneducated streetwalker, and she wanted to make sure her daughter didn't turn into that.

During the winter, it was too cold to be outside, so Lacey would invite the men into the house. She'd tell Ginger to go into her "secret hiding place" for awhile. Instead of having a normal closet in her bedroom like most girls, Lacey had turned Ginger's closet into a castle of sorts, for those who had an imagination. She figured if she couldn't give her little girl the world, she would give her a special place, where she could escape that shit hole of a shack when times were darkest. Inside, Lacey hung a flashlight, which she told Ginger was a magical chandelier, a light only she could see by.

While Lacey was working, Ginger would go in her secret palace and read stories of faraway places, of princes and princesses, and she wondered, as she listened to her mother in the next room, when would her prince come?

Before Ginger was getting ready to leave for the day and go to school, she looked at herself in the mirror. It didn't matter what age she was; this was a lifelong ritual, and she still wondered where her prince was hiding. She was beginning to lose hope that she'd ever find him. This is why she had chosen to study Criminology. Ginger had decided that there were no princes in the world, only people looking to use other people for one reason or another, and she felt that she could at least save and vilify them after death. Death is, after all, life's ultimate betrayal.

Ginger got her books together and headed out to the car. She was particularly proud of her BMW because she'd worked so hard to get it, even if it did cut into her savings a bit. But she figured, she had to live a miserable life right now, so one luxury was fine.

Out of curiosity, Ginger peeked up the street to see if the strange car from last night was still in the parking place, it wasn't. Then, something startled her; she looked directly across the street and it was parked right there. She looked long and hard at the empty car. "Maybe the driver just had to run an errand and came back," Ginger thought to herself. "Yeah, that's what happened," she tried to convince herself as she continued to her own car.

~~~

Milton was crouched down in his front seat, terrified again that he'd been seen. He didn't dare pop his head up yet, not until after a slow count of 60. No one was going to stand there for an entire minute looking at the same car, would they? Better make it a two minute count. He hadn't wanted to park right there, but he'd driven up and down the street several times and this was the only parking spot that had opened up. He felt that he had to take it, or risk missing Ginger.

After two minutes to the second, Milton slowly lifted his head back up in the window, like a turtle coming out of its shell. Ginger was on her way down the street to her car with her back to him. He let out a huge sigh of relief, closing his eyes for a moment of peace, during which time he lost momentary sight of his subject, but that was enough. She'd slipped into her car and was going to soon be driving out of sight.

Rather than look for Ginger's figure walking away, now Milton had to look for any car movement and make a quick plan. Quickly, her sedan pulled out of its spot and drove on down the street. Milton followed from a safe distance with two cars between them. It took what seemed like forever to get to her school, then the real challenge started.

Milton had never been to a college campus, filled with people coming and going, who were all chattery and looking for a friend. He wanted none of that. Who needed friends when you had someone you were following. There was simply no time for that. It was during the following weeks that Milton learned the very delicate art of having to follow someone around crowded spaces, a skill which he had Ginger to thank for and which he would use often during the rest of his life.

~~~

After about two months, Ginger still couldn't figure out why she felt so uneasy all the time. She didn't believe in ghosts but thought, "Maybe this place is haunted," which it wasn't of course. The only thing she knew was that there was something that wasn't right. She couldn't put her finger on it, and she couldn't count the nights she stood staring into that damn tree, but she knew something was wrong.

Ginger had begun dating a nice man from her Criminology class who wanted to go into forensics. He was simple, a bit dorky with his glasses, but he loved her. She'd been able to keep her night job a secret from him, because she knew, as with all of her previous relationships that he would leave her as soon as he found out. She was used to this reaction and had learned to only love men a little bit, to the point of them leaving her, but this man, Jared, was different. She thought that he might be her Prince Charming; that he might be the one who would rescue her and take her away from all of this.

Her life wasn't bad right now, but Ginger just wanted out. She wanted to have a life with an adoring man who gave her children to love and care for, and a big house to clean everyday. These were things she'd dreamed about in that horrid, dingy, dirty sweat-filled shack she'd called 'home' as a child.

~~~

Milton's one gripe with his method of watching was that it was hard to really get to know the people without being involved directly in their thoughts. He'd begun reading lips with Ginger, but it was almost unnecessary because she hardly talked on the phone and had never invited a friend over in all of the weeks he'd been following her. Milton noted what a sad, lonely person she seemed. While he made it a habit not to put many of his own conjectures in his journals, he couldn't help but write:

It's inconceivable to me how someone can stand to live such a life of solitude, having no friends, and no family.

Of course, Milton did not realize the irony in this because in his twisted little mind, Ginger was *his* friend with whom he got to spend his every waking moment. Ginger was the reason he got up in the morning and the reason he hurried through his dreams at night. He felt so sad for her and wanted to help her be happy, but he knew he could do no such thing.

Besides, Ginger's journal was about to come to a close. Between the strip club, the school and his hiding place in the tree, he'd taken thousands of notes on this girl. He knew that her time was fast approaching and within the next day or two, he'd say goodbye to Ginger forever. He was glad the journal had lasted this long because he'd overheard Ginger and her boyfriend Jared talking about their date that was coming up tonight. He was taking her somewhere very special; so special that Milton had had to make reservations that night just to ensure that he was able to get into the restaurant.

Ginger was nearly ready to leave the house for her date. She looked more beautiful than Milton had ever seen her, in fact, he noted:
She radiates.

~~~

That was a compliment Ginger really could have stood to hear for herself. She got to her car, looking around for any suspicious behavior that would explain this nagging feeling, but there was nothing. She got to her BMW and began driving. When she arrived at the restaurant, Jared was already there, holding flowers for her. Daisies, her favorite.

She walked in hesitantly, not sure how to behave at a restaurant this nice, but the moment she walked in, she saw Jared at the table, smiling and waving her over. As Ginger got to the table, he got up and pulled her chair out for her, something she was sure only ever happened in the movies anymore.

Ginger was a ball of nerves, trying to figure out the best time to tell Jared about her secret life, but she didn't want to ruin this evening either. Everything was so beautiful and perfect. So she decided to enjoy herself for awhile.

~~~

Milton had known that Daisies were Ginger's flower of choice since before Jared had even been in the picture, and oddly he resented her boyfriend for the time he spent with Ginger, despite how much better Milton knew her than him. He knew he wasn't supposed to invest any emotion in his subjects, but it was hard with this one.

Once Milton was seated, he found the place at his table that gave him the best view of Ginger and Jared. He was only a few tables away, which he thought was very lucky, and he could still hear them, at least a little bit. Then something very unexpected happened.

"Milton?" he heard from behind him. It was the attorney, Philip Robinson, whom he didn't know well, but hated for calling any kind of attention to his presence. The lawyer was there with his corpulent wife who had slathered on way too much makeup. Milton thought it a shame because she actually seemed like she had a pretty face under all of those cosmetics. Mr. Robinson was a large man himself, with a booming voice and a contagious personality, making it impossible to miss him.

"Shit," Milton thought. He tried to lightly respond and shoo Mr. Robinson away, but that just wasn't possible with this intolerably friendly man.

"Are you here with a young lady, m'boy?" Robinson asked.

"No I'm actually waiting for a *man* to arrive. My lover," Milton hastily added. If there was anything that would make this traditional lawyer go away, it was the prospect of gay love.

"Oh I see, well, uh, um, you, you just have a good time then," Mr. Robinson said with a wave of his hand, as if just hearing the word "gay" could infect him.

"Thank you. I'm sure I will," Milton said with a wink.

He couldn't be positive, but he thought he saw Mr. Robinson wince as he hurriedly walked off to his table.

Milton sighed a sigh of complete relief. He readjusted and got back to watching Ginger and Jared interact. Time went by languorously, as it tends to do at nice places like this one. It was impossible to wrap his head around why people pay more money to sit around for longer, waiting for your food to come out, and then when it did, the plate boasted one tiny piece of shrimp and a few leaves of lettuce. But, this was what Ginger wanted so it was what he wanted, and in turn, what Jared wanted.

~~~

Ginger was still waiting, searching for the right time to tell everything to Jared, but he made it so easy to forget about her life. Everything with him was perfect;

he was perfect. She fought in her own mind against telling him at all, but apparently is showed. Jared asked her if she was alright, adding that she seemed distant tonight. Ginger assured him that she was just fine and reached for his hand to reassure him. Then, Ginger decided in her own mind to put the thought away for tonight and just enjoy herself; the time would come.

~~~

After about an hour, Milton was still watching them, observing, but he didn't realize that he was being observed as well. Mr. Robinson suddenly made another appearance.

"I hope you don't mind m'boy, but the Mrs. and I noticed you were still alone. There's nothing worse than being stood up and being alone in front of people you know, so we've asked our waiter to move us over here to your table. How's that sound?" Mr. Robinson said with a mighty bellow and a clap to Milton's back.

"Oh, uh, uh," Milton was not able to grapple with what had just happened, but he wanted no reason for people to look his way. So he acquiesced. Mr. Robinson plopped right down in front of him, in his line of sight to Ginger. Bastard. Milton was forced to adjust and settle for a slightly less clear view of the object.

"So, did your mother know you were, uh, *homosexual*?" Mr. Robinson asked. This lawyer had never been shy and said exactly what was on his mind so this abruptness did not shock Milton in the slightest.

"Well, he was my roommate in the institution," he began hastily lying, and embellishing. "He had this beautiful body, and we were together all the time, it just sort of happened."

"Uh huh, I see," Mr. Robinson said, obviously uncomfortable, but looking for more to the story.

"So you weren't *born* this way then?" he asked.

"Well I can't say for sure. All I know is that I love men." Milton said this last part a bit too loudly because he got a couple odd looks from surrounding tables. Luckily, Ginger was not one of them. He had to find a way to make Mr. Robinson more uncomfortable, to get him out of here. Then the great, giant lawyer leaned in close to talk to him.

"You know, I have some people who would be happy to pray for you, Milton, to, you know, help you be *normal* again."

"What do you mean?" Milton asked. "I am normal."

"No, no, you're really not," he began, "The love between one woman and one man is normal, but two men loving each other is not the way God intended it to be," Mr. Robinson stated. His lump of a wife sat there nodding in agreement.

Milton leaned in even closer, and whispered, "So, I suppose you haven't told your wife about all your little interns then, have you?" He wasn't sure that Mr. Robinson had any mistresses, but Milton had met men like him before, and it always seemed to be true. Mr. Robinson's reaction confirmed Milton's suspicion.

Just as Mr. Robinson's face turned bright red, and he looked like he was about to punch Milton square in the face, there was a scream from Ginger's table. Milton looked quickly, furious that he had missed what caused this outburst. Then he saw it.

Jared was on one knee, on the floor in front of her, holding a small velvet box with an even smaller ring.

~~~

Ginger didn't care about the size of the ring. She had never thought of marrying Jared, nor had they ever talked about it, but now that the opportunity had presented itself, she thought, "Why not!"

She sat there, staring at him on one knee, like her dreams as a little girl were all coming true.

~~~

Ginger said yes and they hugged and kissed. Everyone in the restaurant clapped for them, except Milton. He was completely dejected that he'd missed the biggest event to happen in Ginger's life since he began following her around. While the Robinsons were still looking at the scene the couple was making, Milton threw a $100 bill on the table and walked away.

Once Milton was gone, Mr. Robinson turned back to talk to him, saying, "See, now that's what love is supposed to look li –" but he stopped short when he realized Milton was gone. He'd disappear and left behind some money. Mr. Robinson feared Milton was going to a bath house somewhere on the seedy part of town, but their third course had just arrived and suddenly, he couldn't care less.

~~~

The entire drive home, Ginger was a bundle of nerves. Here was this man who loved her, who really, really loved her and wanted to spend his life with her. How anyone could really want to spend the rest of their life with one person was beyond her. She couldn't see herself doing it, but she didn't want to be alone either. It was this fear that made her say 'yes.'

It was also this fear that kept her from telling Jared about her true occupation this whole time. Apparently, it was obvious that she'd lost herself deep in thought, because Jared took her hand, kissing her shining ring finger, and said, "You okay? You've been quiet since we left the restaurant."

Ginger tried to snap out of her flood of thoughts and enjoy the present. "Oh! Yes! I'm more than okay. It's just – this was a big surprise! I'm still trying to wrap my head around it." It wasn't entirely a lie.

"I know it was sudden," Jared started explaining, "And I don't want you to feel pressured. If you're having any doubts…"

"No. None whatsoever," Ginger responded, then smiled to reassure Jared. "Just taking it all in."

He pulled up to her apartment building, and leaned in to kiss Ginger goodnight. But without thinking, she pulled back blurted out the truth. It was one of those moments that she could see happening, but couldn't do anything to stop it.

"I'm a stripper." She abruptly said as she pulled away

from him.

The perplexed look on Jared's face said it all. It was like he was staring at a picture, trying to make out just what it was a picture of exactly. Ginger felt his stare, but more than anything she felt fear. Fear that she'd be alone forever and would lose the one person who'd committed himself to her.

"You mean you *were* a stripper, right?" Jared asked, trying to make sense of what had just happened.

Ginger hung her head, ashamed. "No, I *am* one."

"No, but you're a student. You said you were studying all those nights," Jared rationalized to himself.

Ginger just shook her head. She saw him slipping away, quickly. She panicked.

"I'm not a stripper anymore though!" Ginger exclaimed. "I'm giving it up! I want to have a life with you! I want to get married and have a family! I want all of that."

There was an excruciating silence that Ginger thought would suffocate her, that she would die of silence before she had a chance to see this play out; she literally thought her heart stopped.

"So, all those times... You lied to me," Jared was finally fitting the puzzle together.

"It was for your own good. I knew you'd never give me a chance but that we'd be perfect together. I just needed you to see," Ginger continued to plead.

"You lied to me..." became Jared's mantra in the dark of the car.

Ginger finally realized she'd lost. There was no fight left in her. As Jared blankly stared straight ahead, Ginger gave him a little kiss on the cheek. "You need some time to think about this." She began getting out of the car, then took one look back inside before shutting the door. "I love you," she said, and she walked up her stairs. Jared was still staring straight ahead, holding onto the steering wheel trying to figure out what had just happened.

~~~

Milton, of course, saw the whole thing. He wasn't in his tree, because the car was in front of the apartment building, but he saw it all take place, like a bad film. The kind where you're just waiting for a happy ending. He knew he wouldn't be around to see the third act though. His time with Ginger was almost up. He watched from his car, and with his pocket binoculars he could see all of their facial expressions. He couldn't help but feel a pang of joy when Ginger left crying. It wasn't that Milton was in love with her, but it was a type of crush, like a crush you have on your favorite television character; it was a special kind of happiness knowing that she was his to watch again, even if for only a short time.

Jared eventually drove off, slow and steady. Milton took his chance and shot up into his tree. He had to see Ginger and make sure she was okay. When he got up into the tree, and peered into her room, he was not surprised. Ginger had buried her face into the pillows on her bed and she was sobbing; the type of crying where your body convulses. After awhile she surfaced, her face red and puffy and her makeup smeared and running all over the place, like a canvas that's been left in the rain.

Milton had never seen her look such a mess. He made little notations as the night went on, each one bringing him closer to the end of his journal. As he was on his last page, Ginger was sitting on her bed, as she had been for awhile, staring off into space. Then with a sudden and rapid movement, she got up and began packing, Milton didn't know what for, but it was obvious what she was doing. With the end in sight, Milton tried to take notes as accurately and sparingly as possible. It wasn't much use. Just when things were getting interesting, their time had to end.

Milton reluctantly climbed out of the tree, not knowing what to do or where to go from here, except to get in his car and drive home. He was furious that he couldn't see what Ginger's plan was. He lamented over the times when he was too wordy for the sake of passing the time. But, in his true obsessive compulsive ways, Milton was mostly worried that Ginger would leave and never have a chance to see Milton's flower that he would deliver the next day. He didn't know why, but he had this feeling she was going to take off.

Milton had considered getting a florist to deliver the flowers, so that there was no chance of him being seen, but that seemed too impersonal, especially at a time when Ginger was so fragile like this. He finally decided he'd go to Ginger's early in the morning and bring her one of her favorite flower, a daisy. When ever she received them, he'd noted:

Her eyes light up like candles catching fire.

~~~

Ginger was distraught. She realized that she may have just ruined her one chance at happiness; that she was now alone, and it was all because she wanted to absolve herself of some guilt. Even the feeling that someone was watching her was somehow gone. She felt completely alone and knew what she had to do.

As a kid, Ginger's mother moved them from town to town often. It was a occupational hazard, her mother would tell her every time that she asked why they had to go. As a child, Ginger didn't understand what that meant, but it made perfect sense as an adult. Rather than facing loneliness and the awkward memories that everyone is forced to face from the places in which they live, Ginger decided that she had to go. She was going to run away to a town where no one knew her, and where they had a lot of strip clubs. Her mother had taught her that a benefit of being in the "hospitality" line of work was that people, men especially, "always needed to be taken care of."

Ginger knew the vicious cycle would begin again: boy meets girl, boy falls in love with girl, girl reveals she's an exotic dancer, boy runs away. But she felt that she had no choice in the matter; running away was all that she knew, and the only way she could deal with sadness.

Ginger's mother also taught her that when you move somewhere new, you leave all of the feelings and memories behind and get to make new ones. Ginger knew this wasn't true, but her heart hurt so badly that she desperately wanted to believe her mother's words. She stayed up all night, packing all her things and sorting what she didn't need. She could only take what would fit in her car, especially since she had no idea where she was headed.

The way that Ginger's mother used to pick their next home was by choosing a city that started with the letter their last city ended with. So from New York, they moved cross-country to Klamath Falls, and from there they were off to Sacramento, and from there they went to Oklahoma City, and from there they went back across the country to Indianapolis. It didn't matter if it was a town or a city, her mother knew they'd be in need of "hospitality" services. Ginger sat down with a map, surveying her options. She eventually decided on a place about 1,000 miles away that she'd never been to before, but had heard great things about it. She thought it would be the perfect place for new memories and a fresh start.

By the time the sun rose, Ginger had a plan and was moving all her things into her car. She couldn't bear to stay and hear Jared's official breakup with her; it would crush her and she knew it. She had loved living in this city though. So before she left for good, never to return, she wanted to have breakfast, just one more time, at the little café down the street. The one she adored so much. She rarely got to eat there, but some mornings, when the air was crisp, she'd lightly bundle up and head over to her favorite place for some pancakes. "This seems like the best way to leave," she thought, "On a happy note rather than a sad one."

Milton had risen early as well, eager to get over to
Ginger's and leave her a note before she did anything
too drastic. He wrote her a heartfelt letter, similar to
the one he'd written before, last time he let Caitlin go,
and headed over to her place.

There was no need to speed, but Milton definitely felt
like he was in a hurry. If Ginger was doing what it
looked like she was doing, she was about to skip town
and Milton couldn't let her until he'd officially said
goodbye.

When he got there, Milton saw Ginger loading up her
car, packing it full to the very top. Just as he thought,
she was leaving. He had to find a way to her
apartment to leave the flower before she went away
for good. Then, as luck would have it, he saw her load
a basket of clothes into her car, turn and walk up the
street towards the cafe.

Once Ginger was halfway there, Milton hastily got his
note and single flower together, and ran across the
street, in an almost catlike way, making no noise. He
ran up the stairs, two at a time, until he got to the
apartment. He hadn't been this close to it in ages, not
since he first tried picking the lock and got scared off

when someone exited their apartment. After all of the rush getting there, Milton took his time laying out the flower and the note in a meaningful, emotional way; something that would really catch her eye.

Once everything was placed exactly the way he wanted, he fled down the stairs in the same hurry that he had run up them, and back to his car. Then he waited for Ginger to come home. Ten minutes went by, then twenty, then, just when he was starting to get impatient, she came walking up the street. Her gait wasn't strong and assured like it normally was. This was the walk of someone who had been defeated. Her head was hung and she meandered back to the apartment, kicking imaginary rocks along the way. Milton wished more than anything that he had his journal right then. He watched as she went up the stairs and waited for her reaction when she came back down.

As Ginger walked back to her apartment for the last time, hundreds of memories came flooding back to her. She still held onto the hope that Jared would forgive her, that he'd still want to be with her, but she couldn't wait around for him to come back. She walked up her stairs to get one last look at her home, the place she had lived in longer than any other. She was sad to be leaving, but staying would only be worse. As she neared her door, she saw something on the floor in front of it. She walked faster, realizing it was a daisy. Jared always brought her daisies, and he was the only one who ever had. How could she have missed him? How long ago had he been here? Then she saw the note.

She wasn't sure if a note was a good or bad thing, and she was scared to pick it up. After staring at it for a minute or two, she quickly reached down, grabbed it, and hastily opened it. Her eyes scanned frantically, trying to ascertain the message without taking the time to read the whole thing. She was just too anxious though, and had to read it, line by line.

~~~

My darling,

Milton never did call her by Ginger real name, but felt it would be disrespectful to let her know at this point in their relationship so he left the salutation as such.

The note continued:

I've enjoyed these past months more than you know. From the moment I saw you, I knew you had to be a part of my life, and you've been one of the very best parts. I know this may be hard, but I can never see you again. This is the end of me and you.

I'll remember you always...

As she read on, Ginger slumped further and further down the wall, eventually collapsing on the floor in a pile. The one man she'd loved, who she'd seen a future with, who had treated her like a princess rather than a piece of meat, she'd ruined it.

Before she knew what was happening, Ginger was sobbing on the floor in the hallway of her apartment building. She caught her breath finally, after what seemed like forever, and regained her strength to move on. That was it. Jared had thrown in the towel and she was positive she had to leave, and get a fresh start. Grabbing the note and the daisy, Ginger opened her door to say goodbye to the apartment she loved. She didn't go back inside, but rather gave it the once over, so as not to start the waterworks again.

Locking the door, she went back downstairs and out to her car. Before she got into the driver's seat, she carefully placed the note and the flower under her front tire. Ginger got in her car, started it, and drove off to her next city, leaving behind the crushed flower and note.

~~~

When Milton saw this, he was shocked and stunned. He wished so badly he could follow Ginger – what an interesting person she had so quickly become – but it was not to be. After watching her drive out of his sight, he sighed loudly to himself, as if letting go of the final bits of Ginger that he held onto. No sooner had he done that than Jared's car came screaming up the street. He clumsily parked in the spot where Ginger had just been parked.

Astonished, Milton watched as Jared flung his door open and frantically ran up the stairs of the apartment, yelling Ginger's name and wearing a big stupid grin on his face. Milton knew that grin would be gone very soon, and possibly for a very long time. He waited for Jared to come back down.

Instead, something very odd happened. Milton saw Jared walk up to Ginger's window, which was visible to the street only if the person was standing right against it. Milton quickly grabbed his binoculars, too excited to care about anyone seeing him. There were tears rolling down Jared's face, and he wore a look of sadness and despair. He kept looking up and down the street, searching for any sign of Ginger, but there was none. She was gone.

Milton thought for a moment that Jared might be about to jump, but he detected a bit of fear in the man's expression. After several minutes, Jared turned back into the apartment, and Milton put his binoculars down.

Jared moped out of the apartment, softly crying. He got into his car, but he didn't go anywhere, he just sat there. Milton watched him for awhile, but since he struggled with empathizing, he left. It was difficult to understand why a man would feel those kinds of strong emotions towards anyone, except a man's mother, of course.

Sure, Milton became attached to people occasionally, but nothing that would make him sit and cry in a car. This was something he just didn't understand.

~~~

Outside of Missy's apartment, Milton was enjoying the scenery. Trees lined the street; tall trees that you knew had been there for hundreds of years, or at least decades. He'd arrived early, as he'd learned to do with all of his subjects. Silently sitting, Milton waited outside of the apartment, but he didn't smoke.

Most people would expect a stalker to wait, smoking, passing the time, because that's what they did in the movies, but not Milton. He tried that method once, because he figured maybe Hollywood was onto something, but he quickly found out that it wasn't his style.

It had happened when Milton started following Ginger. She came out of her apartment, running to her car. Flustered by the running, he dropped his cigarette in his own car, and was forced to try and crush the smoldering butt while starting the ignition, as he struggled to follow her, all the while thinking, "Why the fuck can't I be as graceful as the stalkers in the movies?!"

Milton idolized the stalkers in movies; not because they were stalkers, but because he liked stealing techniques from them. He was, however, too daft to realize that these were trumped up versions of stalking, and not at all what it was like in real life. It didn't matter though, because this was how he saw himself.

So, Milton sat, waiting for Missy to come out of her apartment, chewing sunflower seeds.

~~~

Meanwhile, Missy was in her apartment, rushing around. She'd gone straight to sleep the night before, but had woken up at 2am. She rolled over to flop her arm over Jay, but he wasn't there. "Because we've broken up," she reminded herself. First, Missy had started by calling out for him, "Jay." Nothing. So she sat up. Once a person sits up, sleep becomes hopeless. Finding this to be true yet again, she laid back down and cried, wanting nothing more than to fall asleep and wake up to life over a year ago.

The fact that she still cried in the middle of the night for this man frustrated the hell out of Missy, but there was nothing she could do. No magic pill would make this go away. So she drank and smoked. The only conceivable way to fall back asleep in her mind was more alcohol and more weed. She spent nearly everything she had om her vices. It was a surprise she could even afford eat sometimes. Everything was just easier to blame on Jay, she decided, than to face her own problems.

So Missy drank. She never shopped at Trader Joe's for anything except wine. Every time she went in, she was petrified that they would recognize her as the alcoholic wine-o who never left without two bottles of Charles Shaw. All night and all morning Missy struggled to pass the time until finally, Missy realized she was late for the bus, which she took to work most mornings.

Missy hastily threw on fresh clothes, not because hers looked bad, but because they reeked of alcohol and sadness. She found a periwinkle sweater and some jeans that weren't too worn.

The bus was a quiet place filled with people who looked like they had more problems than her, and that's why she liked it. Looking around, Missy saw a man twitching uncontrollably, a woman with so many warts on her face that it was like looking at Medusa, and Missy could feel her eyes turning to stone, unable to look away.

There was a man in a thin tank top, beer belly spilling over his waistline and a tiger tattoo bulging forth through his thick chest hair. The homeless person in the very back corner was her favorite though. It was indistinguishable if this person was a man or a woman, the only thing that was clear was that he was rolling a joint.

Missy envied his brashness, and even contemplated asking him for a few puffs, but then she decided against it.

~~~

Milton had always found following the bus to be so troublesome. Really, he hated it. Missy was his first bus rider and things had been very tricky from the get-go. If she wasn't oblivious, she would have seen the odd car making every stop, and right behind the bus at that. There were too many buses in this city, which meant he couldn't risk rushing ahead because maybe then he'd end up following the wrong one.

That first day, Milton just followed the bus, wondering at every stop if he'd missed Missy. Then, two stops away from the end of the route, Missy exited the bus and Milton was relieved. He noted the event and the stop in his journal.

Exited bus at 9:13am off the 2 line, stop at California St. Walked off looking in handbag. Pulls out paper. Walks up the street, looking at each street sign.

Milton geared up for another day of simplicity. Play, sleep, play, eat, sleep. The childrens' lives were so regimented that there was never room for a surprise. The days blended into one another.

But neither Milton nor Missy knew what this particular day held in store.

~~~

This time, Missy got off the bus, heading for the Richards' home, still hating her life. She wondered why in the world she was a nanny, or why Mrs. Richards cheated so often, or why Mr. Richards didn't care. Would she be like that when she got married? *If* she got married... She wondered all of this as she walked to their home, knowing already what her day would be like.

Missy lit a joint she'd rolled at home as she walked to the house from the bus stop. She figured that she had just enough time to get high, spray perfume, use eye drops and get herself together before going into the house. Not that Mrs. Richards would notice anything anyway.

As she walked into the house, everything seemed normal. The kids were eating breakfast, and Mrs. Richards was getting ready for her yoga class. Missy walked to the table and sat down with the Ben and Franny. She'd stopped announcing herself as she walked into the house long ago, as soon as she realized that Mrs. Richards really didn't give a shit. Anything so long as she didn't have to care for her own children.

"What's for breakfast?" Missy playfully asked Franny.

"Mama made us oatmeal, but the oats are cwunchy," Franny pouted. Both children were playing with their food, not eating it.

Missy was getting pretty hungry. "Do you guys want pancakes?"

"Yeah!!" the children yelled in unison.

Missy got to work on the pancakes and the kids

continued to play with their oatmeal, but now they were smiling, knowing they wouldn't have to eat the slop their mom called "food."

Mrs. Richards came downstairs and saw Missy at the stove. "Oh Missy, thank God you're here. It's been such a stressful morning." The kids kept quietly playing with their food.

"I already made them breakfast," she said.

"I know. The kids wanted something else too."

"Okay, whatever. I have a yoga class to get to. Could you take the kids to the park around noon today?"

"Sure. No problem."

"Great. Bye kids. Kisses." Mrs. Richards was one of those people who thought saying something was the same as doing it. Missy had never in fact seen Mrs. Richards kiss her kids, just say "Kisses" to them.

~~~

During this time, Milton would patiently wait outside for Mrs. Richards to leave. Once her car was gone, he'd creep into the backyard. They had no dog, which was something he was very thankful for. There had been one too many dog run-ins during his time following people. The worst one actually sent him to the emergency room for stitches in his ass. But the Richardses had no dog.

From the spot in the backyard, Milton was able to peer into the house, watching Missy cook and the kids play with their food.

He pulled out his journal.

Slumped over the stove. Cooks with care, but has a lackadaisical demeanor.

Part of how Milton was able to make these journals last so long was that he would wait to make notations. Rather than writing everything Missy did as it happened, he would watch for a few minutes, then recap it very succinctly. This was the only way he could spend the most amount of time with his subjects.

Depending on how interesting the person was, Milton would write in the margins and above the page, where the header belonged. He'd fill every single inch of white space available. However, if a subject was not that intriguing, or if he or she turned out to be impossibly boring, then he'd write his notes much larger than was necessary, and stay within all of the lines, "Because it is orderly," the stalker would tell himself.

Milton loved when exciting, out-of-the-ordinary things happened, however, they took up too much room in the journal. In these situations, he wrote down a lot of details, because remembering the essence of an incident was all in the details. Today was going to be one of those eventful days.

Missy finished the pancakes, played with the kids, and before she knew it, it was time for the park.

~~~

Skipping home from the park with the kids, Missy didn't know which way was up and which was down. She'd gotten particularly stoned and was looking forward to eating. She'd already planned out what she was going to make. She felt like cupcakes and pizza, with lots of vegetables on the pizza of course, to balance out the whole "it's a pizza" thing. She figured if she added pineapple, pepperoni and extra tomatoes, she'd be eating her fruit, protein, and vegetable allotment for this meal, well a sort-of vegetable anyway. She never understood why people got so passionate about whether a tomato was a fruit or not. Was it really worth all that extra brain power? Missy certainly didn't think so. The food pyramid was just a loose guide anyway.

As they finished up at the park and neared the house, Missy heard yelling, which she thought sounded like Mrs. Richards. Approaching with caution, the closer she got, she realized it *was* Ben and Franny's mom. Then there was another voice too. It was Mr. Richards yelling at his wife. How Missy had missed his car in the driveway, she wasn't sure, especially since it was parked sideways.

~~~

Milton had heard the yelling long ago. He'd learned to hear extremely well ever since he got snuck up on by that homeless crackhead in the park — an occupational hazard. Ever since then, Milton could hear everything, even the faintest rustling in the woods behind him, no matter how enraptured he was by what was going on in his stalkees life.

So, Milton had heard the fighting well before Missy approached the house. He'd even been tempted to run ahead and see what the commotion was all about, but he had to see how Missy reacted to the situation.

A game he played with himself was to guess how his subjects would react to things, like if they'd freak out or if they'd play it cool; if they'd clam up or explode. He anticipated Missy would just be observing this one.

He was right.

Holding the kids' hands, she approaches the house. Uneasy, unsure. Milton noted.

~~~

When Missy got closer to the house, she began believing more and more that it was the Richards who were fighting. Then, as she was outside in the front yard, holding the kids' hands on either side of her, she realized that the ruckus was coming from inside the home. The nanny stood there, frozen but also curious. She knew the responsible thing to do was to take the kids back to the park, or anywhere but here. Anywhere.

Yet Missy remained outside, holding the hands of two children, who she felt were more hers than the troubled woman yelling inside. She didn't know what to do. All she knew was that the rest of her stash was inside the house, and it would clearly be necessary .

"Why are mommy and daddy yelling?" Franny asked, as any child would.

"I'm not sure why, Franny," she said as she drifted closer to the house.

Missy reached for the doorknob, and slowly turned it.

As she did so, she and the children tentatively peered into the house. Missy instantly regretted her decision to go inside, but she needed her weed now more than ever. She felt that her life in general sucked, but especially considering these current circumstances, Missy needed her stuff.

As she peered inside through the open front door, not stepping inside quite yet, Missy saw the gardener, lying on the floor, beaten to a pulp. He was moving, but barely, and he was stark naked. Her first thought was that she could see why Mrs. Richards had picked him, despite his lower class. Even bloodied, it seemed like the muscles on his chest rippled just from him breathing, which he was still doing despite being unconscious.

Scattered on the floor around the young man were all of Mrs. Richards' clothes. She was kneeling over his body, trying to attend to him despite the barrage of things that were flying at her from upstairs. Everything from camisoles to hair dryers were being flung over the bannister, which looked down into the living room where the body was lying, with Mrs. Richards' head as the new target.

Upstairs, Missy could see Mr. Richards, completely disheveled, his half-untucked white dress-shirt spattered with blood, his eyes wild. Not one adult seemed to notice the children and Missy creeping into the house.

Missy looked frantically around the room, searching for her purse among the debris. Once she saw it, she darted in, making sure to avoid anything flying through the air. Ben and Franny, meanwhile stood in the doorway, grasping each other tightly, not sure what exactly it was that they were seeing. As soon as she'd found her bag, Missy hurriedly exited the house and took the kids back down the street to the park.

It was quiet for a few minutes until eternally curious Franny spoke up, "Why was Daddy throwing Mommy's clothes downstairs?"

"They were playing a game," Missy answered without thinking. It was a frantic answer that was given more to shut Franny up than to address the situation. Missy just needed to get high. Right. Now.

"And why was that man on the floor?" Ben asked.

"He fell asleep," she said.

"Oh." Ben thought for a moment, "He must be really tired to sleep through that yelling."

Franny laughed. Their mood instantly lifted, as only a child's laughter can make it, but Missy was still coping with what she had just seen, and she knew that coping wasn't going to be easy.

Once they got to the park, Missy sat down in her usual spot and pulled out her Ziploc baggie of pot and zigzags. She began rolling a joint. It was in plain view of anyone on the street and the children, but she didn't care. Any cop would *have* to understand after they saw the mess down the block. So she smoked, and suddenly realized she had a lot of decisions to make.

Should she call the cops? Where would the kids stay tonight? Why had Mr. Richards come home early? Would he kill Mrs. Richards and finish off her lover? Does the gardener need a hospital?

Consumed in thought, and the process of rolling, Missy didn't notice Ben walking over to her. He stood there staring at her for a minute.

"What is that?" he asked, puffing out his tummy and pointing his finger in front of him, at her joint.

Without thinking Missy said, "A joint. It makes you feel better and forget about what's going on."

"Can I try it?" Ben asked. Franny ran up yelling, "Can I too??" Franny had no idea what Ben was talking about, but him trying something that she couldn't was intolerable.

Missy thought for a second, as she looked deep into the cyclops eye of the joint before twisting it off. It couldn't *really* hurt, right? Besides, she couldn't be expected to make responsible decisions after what she'd just seen. "Sure, but it has to be our little secret, okay?"

Both children early nodded their heads, excited to try something forbidden.

After Missy had finished smoking the joint with the kids, she saw a cop car speed by the park towards the house. Instead of feeling paranoid, she felt relieved. After all, she was stuck with these kids, for now, but at least they were calmed down. Before they knew it, the night had come, and the cold came with it. Missy grabbed the hand of each child, and led them back to the house. As they did so, a police car drove by them, with Mrs. Richards in the back.

~~~

This was all too much for Milton. Seeing the Richardses fighting took him back to his childhood, to that moment when his mom and the pool boy were on the roof; the moment that changed his whole life.

He of course wanted to stay and watch what was going to transpire and how Missy would react to it all, but that was entirely out of the question. There was no way he would be able to observe, not in this frame of mind. No way, no how. So he left.

The drive home seemed timeless, not in an eternal way, like it would never end, but in a way that he felt it never happened. He was so consumed with thoughts about his mother that he didn't even pay attention to the road; he was just going through the motions. His body was in the driver's seat, but his mind was decades away.

~~~

After Milton's first girl, Caitlin, he tried following a man for awhile. He thought it might be interesting, to see what another man did throughout the day, to see how he spent his life. Milton knew he himself was not a normal man, but he wasn't quite sure what "normal" *was*. This was to be his test and what would show him how a *man* was supposed to act.

Milton sat on a park bench, pretending to read a newspaper, and watched the people until he found a man who he thought was worthy of following. After a few hours, Milton finally saw a family walk onto the grassy knoll nearby. They were having a picnic, the dad moving between laying out the blanket for his wife, and playing Frisbee with his kid.

In his mind, this was the perfect family. Milton watched them the whole time they were at the park, eating their food, playing games, laying down and snuggling. He was so intent on watching them, that he forgot what he was there for. Then it hit him.

This father was a man. He was, in fact, everything that Milton thought a man should be. So, when the family got ready to leave, Milton quickly gathered his things and readied himself to follow them home.

As they drove, Milton was excited at the prospect of following around a male. A real man. Something he'd been waiting years to experience. However, 'The Experience' turned out to be one of the most disturbing in his life. The compulsion to see his subject through till the end though made it impossible for him to leave.

That first day was fine. Milton followed the family home, and promptly started a new journal. During this day, he discovered the man's name was Johnny. Johnny had a wife named Regina and the kids were John Jr. and Sofia. The family functioned just like Milton envisioned any "normal" family functioning. The kids had bedtimes; Johnny tucked them in, read them bedtime stories, and kissed them on the foreheads before leaving the room. Then, he'd return downstairs with his wife where they chatted before he headed off to bed. All was well in the home. Finally, after the last light had been turned out, Milton left for his house, feeling excited at the prospect of seeing a normal family.

Since he'd chosen to follow Johnny, not the mother, he had the opportunity to see how the real head of the household functions. How he treats his family and goes to work every day, how he plays games with his children in his free time and makes love to his wife at night (yes, Milton watched even when people had intercourse, as it was another part of the human experience that he needed to document). Milton watched in the most scientific way possible though, as though the couple was a part of a clinical study.

Running on only a few hours sleep, Milton got to Johnny's house bright and early. Johnny was just leaving for work when Milton arrived. He watched the kids pile into Johnny's car as they drove away. The car, a new Jaguar, drove for 30 minutes, weaving in and out of traffic on the freeway. Milton documented while driving:

Drives fast and reckless, even with children in the car.

Milton was relieved when the car finally exited the freeway, and wound slowly through the suburban streets. Finally, Johnny pulled up to a school and the kids piled out of the car. Milton watched from a safe distance. Then Johnny was on his way again.

Johnny worked in a large, high-rise building and Milton spent a long time trying to figure out how he was going to get to him, when suddenly, Milton saw the Jaguar fly past him. Milton got into his car as quickly as he could and tried to follow the car. It was tough, but once they began entering the seedy part of town, the traffic died, and Milton had the opposite problem of trying to stay far enough away, after racing to catch up.

Finally the car stopped right in front of what looked like a pub called Cock and Bull. "Odd name," Milton thought to himself, but he watched Johnny walk in. He looked at the clock; it was only 10:30am. After waiting until 10:45am and seeing no sign of Johnny, Milton decided to go in and see have a drink.

"I knew I should never have followed a man," Milton thought to himself as he walked in. He was greeted at the door by a very beautiful, very tall, muscular woman who was clad in a skin tight patent leather bodysuit, wearing a spiked choker. She smiled and approached Milton.

"You look like a bad boy. Who are you here to see?"

Milton had no idea what to say. Since he spent most of his life *watching* other people, he was horrible at *talking* to them.

"Ah, um..." he stammered. "Juliette." His mother's name. He knew he didn't want to see anybody, that he just wanted to find the man. But there was no way.

"Juliette huh? You gonna be her Romeo?" the leather girl said with a wink.

"Ah, yes. No! Yes." Milton was so flustered that he didn't know what to do.

She began to lead Milton down a long, small hallway with red walls to a nondescript room. As she turned the doorknob, suddenly, he couldn't handle it anymore. He rushed outside, leaving Johnny, and any hope of following him in that place, far behind him.

Milton ran out to his car and drove away.

As he started moving, Milton realized he was losing focus and running away from what really mattered: following Johnny. So he circled the block, cooled off, but by the time he got back, Johnny's car was gone. Milton was furious with himself. If he had only been more of a, well, more of a man then he wouldn't have lost Johnny.

Milton wasn't sure why he was so scared of women. It wasn't necessarily the actual woman, but more the thought of having to be with one, rather than just watching her. He did not like that idea at all. Just thinking about this Juliette, whoever she may have been, made him break into a cold sweat while he was driving. He was so overwhelmed that he wasn't even paying attention to the road. All he knew was he was driving. Thinking about women, and he slowly drifted back to his childhood.

~~~

When Milton was in the mental facility, he'd had a friend named Jenny. She was a pretty blonde girl around Milton's age, who he liked because she reminded him of his mother.

Jenny had an odd problem. She loved animals to death, literally. It wasn't in a psychopathic growing-up-to-be-a-serial-killer way, but in a childish way. When she saw a cute little animal, she felt compelled to hug it tightly, squeeze it and show it love the way a three-year-old shows love to her teddy bear. Jenny had killed seven of the family cats before her parents decided she needed to live in this facility. They thought the people here could shock the behavior out of her.

Milton, who prided himself on his spying abilities, would sneak and look in Jenny's window while she was going through treatments. He'd watch the doctor give her a stuffed animal and she'd get so excited. Milton loved the look on her face when she'd get that toy. And then it would happen. She would get too excited. The doctor would try to settle her down, telling her that she was hurting the animal. Jenny would squeal, "But it's just so cute!"

Then it would happen. The doctor would actually shock the shit out of Jenny. She would scream, then you'd see shit running down her leg. She'd cry, they'd hand her another animal, she'd smile and squeeze it, and she'd get shocked again. Jenny couldn't control herself when she saw something cute.

Milton wanted to help Jenny. But he didn't know how. She was only allowed to have those little bears when the doctors were around.

During their free time, Milton would approach Jenny, but she ignored him. She just sat around crying, asking for a new animal.

~~~

Milton floated back to reality and found himself in front of Johnny's office. How he'd navigated there was beyond him, but there he was, right where he needed to be. Johnny parked underground so Milton's only option was to wait for him to go home for the afternoon, so he sat there.

Milton was used to waiting. He'd spent so much of his life sitting and waiting that it didn't even phase him anymore. As he sat outside the office, he began thinking about what he'd experienced earlier, and began to write it down.

Milton was convinced that he no longer liked following a man. This confirmed that he needed to only follow women, and for good reason.

Johnny had gone into some sort of whore house, only it was an insane whore house. The women were too eager and dressed funny. Milton did not approve. Though, he knew he couldn't say this definitively without having actually gone inside and seen what it was that Johnny was doing with that woman. He began to get afraid. What if he had to go back in there?

They'd surely remember him. Maybe he could use a little disguise. Wear a mustache and all. Milton remembered being a child and seeing the gardener with a mustache. Then one day he didn't have it, and Milton did not even recognize the man. He asked his mother who the new gardener was. She looked at the man, smiled, waved and said, "Oh it's the same man. He just shaved."

"Why did he shave it? He looks so odd."

"Because I asked him to," she said while waving and smiling at him, seemingly forgetting that Milton was even there.

So Milton knew the faux facial hair would work, but he would have to be careful if he ate anything. He made a note to himself on his palm, then continued writing in the journal, making sure to be as detailed as possible so as to use up the journal faster.

Johnny likes the whores. While I did not see him with one, I followed him into a brothel full of odd, leather-clad women. I've been waiting outside this office building for nearly five hours. If he is working an eight hour day, I should expect him to leave soon.

But Milton somehow missed Johnny. He waited until the sun was down and night had truly fallen. In fact, he even dozed off a couple times. This is when Milton decided that it may be time to head back to Johnny's home and make notes on the family. He could learn about the man by studying those whom he spent the most time with.

Once he pulled up, Milton was flabbergasted to find that Johnny had already arrived. His interest piqued and Milton instantly slunk toward the house. He needed to hear what was going on. That was the main thing he was missing from his observations up to this point was the audio track to Johnny's life.

Everyone has a soundtrack. Milton considered his own to be classical music. The nocturnes of Chopin and Tchaikovsky. Serene, but dark, since he did most of his work in the dark.

Milton never considered himself in danger, although he crept about in the night. He considered himself to be a shadow, to be something that blended into the night, and that's why he was able to sneak around as he was.

Kneeling underneath a window, Milton poked his head up and peered inside. He found a family, happily sitting at a table. They were laughing and the mother was serving them all dinner. It looked like an antiquated painting of how life used to be before technology took over.

Milton noted this.

Family is eating dinner. They either ignore that Johnny was at the brothel, or they do not know. They are the happiest family I have ever seen.

Milton began to reminisce about his own family, then he caught himself. He frequently found himself sinking into thought, flashbacks, and he had to stop. These would interfere with the work, clearly. But some were too overwhelming to contain. This, luckily, was not. He pushed the thought away and continued observing.

After dinner, the little stereotypes cleaned up and the dad helped his wife put the kids to bed. Milton crept around the house, looking for different windows to spy through. He made notes.

Johnny is talking to his wife. She is dressed down but he is still in his slacks. He is telling her something, which I still can't hear, and she looks upset. He seems to be comforting her slightly. She remains sitting, but he walks towards the door. He grabs his keys and walks out the front door.

As Milton was writing, he began creeping back to his car, reading the situation and knowing that he was going to have to drive somewhere very shortly. As he got to his car, Johnny began backing out of the driveway. Milton slowly followed, sans headlights. They wound through some suburban streets, and Milton wished they would get on a main road so he could turn his lights on again.

After about five minutes, they entered a semi-main road with enough people driving on it to cover up all suspicion. Milton followed Johnny back through the seedy part of town, stopping on the fringe. Johnny got out of his car, which looked very out of place in this lower income neighborhood, and went into a dingy looking house.

Milton parked and walked toward the house. In this area, he did *not* feel like a part of the night, and *did* feel the threat that surrounded him. He didn't worry about the crackheads who were everywhere, willing to suck your dick for a fix, or shank you for your wallet, whichever was easiest.

So Milton wound around the shack, looking for where Johnny had gone. This was the hardest part of following, locating someone once they were inside of a building. He couldn't very well knock on the door and see what happened, ask if so and so was there. So he crept, ignoring the black sedan that was slowly driving by for the second time.

Finally, as he edged toward the back of the house, Milton found his subject. Johnny was completely naked, which Milton noted, having intercourse with someone Milton could not see.

Milton was disturbed by the fact that Johnny was

cheating on his wife, but he had to put those prejudices behind him. He was here to observe, not judge, which he did successfully, until he saw Johnny's partner.

It was a man. Milton grappled with this for a moment, which he berated himself for. He was supposed to be professional, just observing and making notes. It also felt odd because he felt so comfortable with the idea of homosexuals that he'd even pretended to be one to chase off Mr. Robinson. Yet, there was something about the situation he was watching unfold that made him feel embarrassed, sad, and ashamed.

He wrote furiously in his book, trying to fill up as much space as possible, as he tried to suppress the memories.

~~~

When Milton was a boy, in middle school, before he was sent away, he'd noticed that he'd begun developing faster than the other boys. When girls wore short skirts he had to fight furiously to hide his excitement in class.

Then one day, after soccer practice, things changed for him. Milton's coach had said he should stay later to practice privately with him. One-on-one. He was the goalie, so the coach was going to shoot at him for awhile. By the time Milton got to the locker room to shower and head home, the other boys were gone.

Milton was already awkward about his body, with all of it's constant changes, so he undressed quickly and hopped in the shower to rinse off. He was actually kind of glad the boys were gone because he was able to relax. The showers were usually such a loud, raucous place, with towels snapping and the overwhelming smell of sweat permeating everything. Having lived at home with his mother for so long, Milton didn't handle uncleanliness very well. He could tolerate it, but it bothered him something fierce.

Milton was happy to have the locker room to himself, until he heard the footsteps.

They were heavy steps, not those of his teammates. Coach rounded the corner.

"Mind if I join you?" Coach beamed at Milton.

"Uh sure. I'm almost done anyway," Milton said hurriedly.

"No rush. I wanted to talk some strategy with you," Coach said.

"Sure," Milton hesitantly answered back.

The showers were a large area with various shower heads. No one had any privacy in there. It was a bullpen of shower heads, and the coach was standing at the entrance, right next to Milton.

He'd had the whole shower area to choose from and he chose to be right next to the young boy.

"Good practice today," Coach said, staring Milton in the face.

Milton made it a point not to catch his gaze, but he felt it on him. "Thanks," Milton squeaked out.

"You know, I can help you get into a college to play soccer," Coach told him.

Milton would have loved nothing more than to play a college sport. Then all of the girls would love him for sure. "Really?" he perked up. Only something horrible happened just then. As most young boys get erections without warning, the thought of college girls had suddenly aroused Milton, and the coach took notice.

What happened next was something that Milton grappled with for the rest of his life. He never told a soul, always believing it was his fault, that if he had only been able to think of things more objectively, then Coach would have never made advances. His inability to control his body had given Coach "the signal" and everything else that happened was a blur.

Milton was never the same after that. He quit the soccer team and gave up on all manly exploits.

With no father around, he felt lost as to what men were supposed to do. He looked up to athletes but they cheated on their wives, which Milton found abhorrent. Or there were the cookie-cutter families on TV, but Milton knew those families were fake. They weren't something you could duplicate because those people had been cast to play those perfect parts. In real life, Mr. Cleaver couldn't be that good of a guy.

As an adult, Milton also wondered if Coach ever did that to any other boys. He hoped not, when he realized that just saying something to Principal could have changed someone else's life.

This was too much emotion for Milton to deal with, so whenever this train of thought crept into his head, he quickly pushed it out, and focused on the task at hand.

What was done was done, and it was too late to go back now.

~~~

As Milton watched Johnny and his lover, the stalker reminded himself that this was consensual, and he wrote that fact down, almost as a reinforcement for his own psyche, as he was struggling with the fact that he had to finish out this journal at all. He didn't care that Johnny was bisexual, but he cared that he lied to his wife and his perfect little family, a family that Milton had longed to be a part of the day that he saw them. But not anymore. His dream of the perfect family was crushed.

"This was no man," Milton thought to himself. "Men don't do this to the people they love."

Originally, Milton had excitedly set out to follow the 'quintessential man;' someone who he could look up to. Milton had planned to reread *this particular* journal often, whenever he wanted to know what a man would do in a certain situation.

This was not what he thought was going to happen.

So Milton wrote in furious detail, and in large print, everything that occurred between Johnny and the man, even how happy they both looked together. He noted that the couple looked happier than Johnny did with his wife.

He just wanted his time with Johnny to end...

~~~

Night had fallen, and the police had cleared out. All the while, Missy, Ben, and Franny had sat in the park, smoking and thinking about anything that didn't have to do with what was really going on at the house.

Mrs. Richards found Missy and the children sitting together, not taking the time to realize they were stoned, because her own plight took precedence.

"Missy, sorry you had to see all that. Can I give you ride home?" Mrs. Richards said.

Missy nodded. "The kids —" she started.

"Oh, they'll just go right to sleep in the back seat and be fine, right kids?" She cheerfully looked at her kids who, with their half closed eyes certainly looked like they would be falling asleep soon.

They headed back to the house. Missy sat in the car, and Mrs. Richards walked Ben and Franny up to bed. Missy sat there wondering how people like this women were allowed to exist let alone have children. People who have no regard for anyone but themselves. There was no way this kind of complete narcissism should be okay. She sat there pondering this until Mrs. Richards came down to the car and got in, smiling and smelling amazing.

How were people this crass and callous brought into the world? It didn't matter. At this hour, she was Missy's only ride home.

The whole drive, Mrs. Richards tried to be chipper and lighthearted, as if nothing had happened at all. As if Missy hadn't seen a man nearly beaten to death in their living room. As if no one was aware that she was having at least one affair.

Missy gave one-word answers, trying hard not to like this woman, who was quite enchanting when she wanted to be. This was Missy's first time seeing her in this light; as a person that she could actually spend time with, instead of the shallow cougar that she typically portrayed herself as. This was not lost on Missy; the drive both flew by and seemed endless at the same time.

~~~

Milton hated following Mrs. Richards. She was truly an awful driver. He could only imagine the drivel she tried to talk to Missy about. Missy, this intelligent, albeit misguided person had to listen to Mrs. Richards for that entire long drive, and thinking about that made Milton sad.

In cases like this, Milton had to remind himself that he was writing his observations of *Missy* and not *Mrs. Richards*, who frankly sometimes seemed much more interesting, no matter how much he despised her.

The fact that Mrs. Richards was so blatantly and unabashedly selfish was almost to be admired. Imagine how much happier we'd all be if we did exactly what we wanted with no concern of repercussions. That was a trait of a sociopath though, so Milton quickly pushed the want out of his mind.

Mrs. Richards dropped Missy off, pushing a $100 bill into her palm and apologizing for what had transpired. Swearing up and down that "I love my children, and my husband of course, but sometimes life is confusing. You're too young to understand that though."

Missy listened, numb to the words. Quite frankly, she didn't care. While she didn't want anything bad to happen to Ben and Franny, they were a paycheck. Whether or not they had a good mother was not her concern. What she was really worried about was the fact that she would once again be going to bed alone, without anyone to tell about her hellish day.

That was something Missy was not ready to cope with. She looked at the $100 knowing it would all be spent on a bar tab, or better yet, at a liquor store, because now was no time to be around people. Now was a time to sit alone, and think about how you have fucked up your life, your relationships and everything else you wanted. It was a time to stare out the window at the giant city spread out around you and wonder if anyone even cares about you. If there's anyone who thinks about you, who even knows you exist. Who would miss you if you weren't there.

Of course, this is nothing that the beautiful Mrs. Richards would understand though.

Missy got out of the car, and walked to her door. She fumbled for her keys, planning on walking to the door, waving to Mrs. Richards, letting her know she got in okay, then leaving immediately and going to the liquor store. As soon as Missy slammed the car door shut, Mrs. Richards gave her a cute little finger wave, then took off, speeding down the street. Missy's fear had been confirmed, no one gave a damn about her.

~~~

Milton sensed her sadness as she stood dejected on the stoop of her building, looking after a car that was long gone. While Milton knew he was to stay detached, that sad look was too familiar to him. He'd seen it before on Jenny.

As Milton grew older, he began to realize that Jenny had been his one true love. Not in those traditional terms of course, because "love" was such an intangible concept (especially in a mental hospital), but she had been the one person he longed for, who he desperately wanted to make happy, and who he would have done anything for.

When Milton saw Jenny after her shock therapy sessions, and she was so teary eyed and sad, he physically hurt for her. There was a rock in his gut, like gas pains, only worse. It was as though if he could hurt badly enough, she would be okay. But he knew it would never happen like that.

Jenny sat there, across the table, murmuring the names of different animals as she stared into space. Kitty. Bunny rabbit. Puppy. Every single one made her smile slightly, which was quickly replaced with a few silent tears. Sit she for hours, naming adorable animals over and over again, and quietly crying.

After a few months, they had finally shocked the soul out of Jenny. She no longer said the names of cute fluffy animals, she just stared into space, thinking about who knows what. Milton hoped it was him that she filled her ghost brain with, but he knew it wasn't. It was time for Jenny to leave the facility.

She gathered her things to go, and Milton saw her.

"Are you leaving?" he asked her, shocked.

"Yes. They say I'm well and I can go home," Jenny emptily replied, as though she were a robot.

Milton was frantic. "Well, but what about the animals? You don't want to play with them anymore?"

"No. Animals are for looking, not for touching," she said with no inflection; just repeating what she was told by the doctors.

"Are you sure you don't want to hold them just one more time? I have a kitty stuffed animal in my room," he lied, but he had to try anything to keep her here, near to him. Without her, he thought the sadness would drive him insane.

Jenny thought for a moment. Then finally, "No. Kitties are not for playing. I don't want to touch them."

Finished packing, Jenny stood to look at him. "Goodbye Milton." It was a moment he would never forget. In her eyes he could see that Jenny was far, far away. It was the blankest, loneliest look he had ever seen. As if she didn't have a friend in the world.

Jenny grabbed her suitcase and headed out. Milton memorized everything about her walking away from him, knowing that he would never see this lovely creature again. As she turned the corner to leave the building, Milton felt a tinge of sadness, remembering the moment she walked away, then composed himself and moved on. Feeling any kind of sadness for more than a few seconds wasn't permitted, according to the rules he'd made up for himself. It wasn't worth it.

~~~

Milton looked at Missy, standing there on the curb, and made note of her emptiness. As he did so, he realized he was on the last page of his journal. He decided to draw it out, to spend as much time with this lonely girl as possible.

So, the stalker followed his subject down the block to the liquor store. She stared at the wall of liquor behind the cashier. The man just looked back at her, then said, "What do you want?"

Missy sighed, "Something as mind numbing as Jaeger,

but something that doesn't make me feel like I'm missing out on a party."

"JD's always a safe choice."

"That' what I was leaning towards anyway," She said with a sigh, handing him the cash.

"You want the big bottle?" he said surprised, looking at the $100 bill.

"Yes. Just for little ole' me," she said with a feeble smile.

He hesitated before giving it to her, weary of the fact that based on her appearance she might end up drinking the whole thing, and get alcohol poisoning. Then again, that big bottle of Jack had been up there awhile.

The cashier gave it to Missy, and she left without a word, tearing off the packaging around the cap without hesitation as she walked outside. The way she saw it, if she got arrested for drinking in public, at least someone would be paying attention to her.

~~~

So, Missy headed back to the apartment, unknowingly passing Milton on the way. She'd already taken the equivalent of four shots by the time she got upstairs, where she proceeded to drink more. She wasn't sure what she wanted.

Would she drink enough to get drunk and pass out? Enough to warrant her calling her ex, pleading for help after drinking too much? Or enough to die of alcohol poisoning, leaving her body for her landlord to find after a strong, horrible odor came wafting down from her apartment. Surely rumors would spread that the building was haunted and make Missy famous after death. It would be more attention than she ever got in life.

Missy didn't know what she wanted. All she knew was that she liked the numbness that was coming over her, and she wanted it to continue. She wanted to be so drunk that she couldn't feel feelings.

~~~

Milton wrote the last page, which was full of Missy's misery and self-loathing. He wished things had ended on a happier note, but it seemed like he would have to remember her like this. Had she known she was being watched, Missy might have put on a better performance, but then again, Missy wasn't the type who was given to attention. She liked certain people to notice her, but on the whole, that wasn't her thing.

So Milton closed the journal, got into his car and made the long drive home, mentally breaking up with Missy the whole way. He felt for the girl, knowing she was just lost and lonely, and knowing he felt the same way often. If he hadn't found his calling long ago, then he might still feel that way. Who knows.

By the time he got home, Milton was tired. He had found Missy to be difficult to part with, so he relied on a method he'd developed long ago. When he wanted to part with someone who he found likable, he had to tell himself all the awful things about that person. So the whole way home, he thought up every negative thing he could about Missy. By the time he went to put the journal away, he just tossed it onto the stack, loathing his subject at this point. Then he went off to bed.

~~~

The next day, Milton rose a bit later than usual. He allowed himself this luxury in between subjects. He only got this one day to sleep in, and he didn't know how long it would be until the next one. Part of him hoped it would be a long time, because that meant that he had found someone interesting to follow, but when it was only about a month between sleep-in days, he was happy with that too. It meant he'd found someone he did not enjoy, but that he was getting better at taking detailed notes. There was a positive to everything.

On this sleep-in day, Milton would wake up when his body told him to, then cook a grand breakfast. Eggs, bacon, biscuits, pancakes, fruit, and he would eat it all. It made him think of when he was a kid, and Mother would cook large breakfasts. It usually meant she was in a good mood because his father was gone.

Milton's mother would cook all kinds of food. She was really a very good cook, despite the fact that she didn't do it often. She would encourage her son to eat everything on his plate, and he would, past the point of bursting. Then he would go read a book, because he was too full to play outside.

So, on these special days off, Milton allowed himself the luxury of eating a very large breakfast. He'd browse through the newspaper, see what the scuttlebutt was. Then he would start preparing for his next encounter.

Since it was a nice day outside, Milton thought that he might sit at an outdoor café and see who he ran into there. Sitting at these places always made Milton wish that he was going off to find a subject in another country. Somewhere fancy like France or Spain. The thought had crossed his mind frequently, but Milton found it impractical. He only knew English, so getting around would be difficult, and he would have to spend time studying the city before he could properly find someone. No, it would be a tremendous waste of time.

Once he sat down at a café in the city, Milton began to take note of the people around him. He was wearing sunglasses and had brought a newspaper so as to seem inconspicuous. His journal was tucked away in his coat in case he found someone who he decided was the perfect subject right away. There was a slim chance of this happening, but a person can never be too prepared.

After a few hours, Milton began to grow weary of that corner café. Maybe it wasn't as great of an idea as he had thought. So, he gathered his things to leave, and pulled out his wallet to pay what had now become quite a large bill, when he saw her.

A blonde woman sat down right at the table across from him. She was the most beautiful creature that Milton had ever seen. Her hair was just below shoulder length with soft, natural looking waves. Her lips were a rosy red, and she had a button nose that was of the perfect size to be adorable and not over-buttony. Her giant blue eyes seemed to be smiling at him, although he was wearing sunglasses and knew she couldn't see him staring. Milton's eyes crept lower. She was wearing a floral shift dress, with very ample breasts. They were so big in fact that Milton found his gaze lingering there longer than was necessary, not for any sexual reason, but because they were so big and perfect that he couldn't believe it. As if they had been crafted just for her.

This was the woman of Milton's dreams, which presented him with a problem: would her appearance be a distraction if he were to follow her? Milton didn't know the answer, but he did know that he needed to be around this woman. He needed to hear her talk, to smell her, to know what she was like, he needed to know why she was at this café right now. He needed all these answers, and a few minutes after he pulled out his journal to begin writing, a man sat down across from her.

~~~

Milton didn't care about this Rico Suave character, because he knew that nothing romantic would likely come from following this blonde woman, so he was content to just be near her. To just know what made her tick. He knew that what he would find out about her was more than any man would be able to, because Milton was an observer. He knew how to read into the little things, like a look, or a laugh. For example, he knew that this woman was nowhere near as into the man sitting across from her as the man was into her. And this Milton noted it in the journal he'd just pulled from his coat.

Since Milton had begun to pack up right as she sat down, he hurriedly fumbled with his journal, so that he could document all of his first impressions. Unfortunately, in his bumbling, Milton had drawn some attention to himself, and he tried to play it cool.

Once the journal was out, and he was sitting again, the stalker wrote down his impressions so quickly that it would even be difficult for Milton to decipher. He calmed himself and began writing down more useful observations.

Smiles warmly at man, and daintily shakes hand. It's a flimsy handshake. She doesn't get up when he arrives.

~~~

Norma liked Guy enough, but he just wasn't right for her. Sure, he bought her a lot of nice things, but he didn't challenge her. She felt like he was too in awe of her. She loved the attention, in fact she craved it, but he was too busy to give her enough of what she needed, and when they finally did get together, he'd just stare at her, hardly engaging in conversation. Later, Guy would always apologize profusely for not being able to talk to her when she'd called him. He was in a meeting or on a conference call or making a presentation.

It was always something that sounded important, but Norma didn't care and never listened. She had important whims too, and she needed someone who would be there right when she wanted him. Just today, Norma had thought to herself that maybe she wasn't good enough to be an actress, and she should just quit. So she called Guy, who would undoubtedly talk to her in his calm, soothing voice and tell her that she was beautiful and talented and people loved watching her on stage. He would reassure her that she was on the right career path, even though she hadn't landed a major role yet.

But Guy didn't pick up when she called, and that's why he was here right now. There had been no mistaking that Norma was upset with Guy, annoyed more than upset, and now he was grovelling, telling her he was sorry. Guy was promising that as soon as he closed this deal, he would take her to Fiji for a week. She was only half-heartedly listening because at this point, Norma had spotted a man at the table across from them. He was a slight man, mousy with dull brown hair, who tried to act like he was reading a newspaper, but it was obvious he was watching her. Then, what seemed like an hour later, when Guy was done with his spiel and on his way back to the office, the mousy man was re-reading the same section of the paper. Norma knew she should have been listening to what Guy had to say before he left, but what did it matter. She wouldn't be with him for much longer, and she saw a new prospect on the horizon.

Norma liked that the mousy man had hung around this long and was secretly watching her. If Guy couldn't give her the attention she craved, it seemed this man might. She knew it wasn't ladylike for a woman to approach a man, so she didn't, and she knew with the looks she'd been giving him that he'd come over to her any minute.

But the man didn't. Norma sat there coyly drinking her tea, drawing out the process. It was very cold by the time she decided to leave, which she decided to do when her confidence was faltering. If the mousy man hadn't come over to her, maybe he wasn't interested after all and she'd misread his signals. She hadn't been to the gym in a couple days. Maybe she was carrying more water weight in her face and wasn't looking as great. Who knows, but she had to get out of there before she had anymore bad thoughts about herself.

Her therapist had taught her that bad thoughts were what made her perform poorly, and Norma had an audition tomorrow. She could only afford to feel superior, desired, and important.

So, Norma paid her bill, then she sat there for a few

moments, unable to push thoughts of inferiority out of her head. The debate was whether she should leave and accept that this man genuinely had no interest in her. Or she could walk right over to his table, plop herself down and force him to talk to her.

There was a great risk in this. What if the mousy man really had no interest in her and he turned her away. This would be a far bigger blow to her confidence than just leaving and *assuming* that he had no interest in her. The choice was impossible, but she decided the unknown was worse than the known. At least she would find out what his deal was.

Mustering up all of her confidence, Norma walked right over to the man's table, and he again put the newspaper in front of his nose, pretending not to see her. As soon as he made eye contact, Norma knew she had made the right choice.

~~~

Milton was startled to say the least. One minute he had been mentally preparing to leave, and the next this beautiful woman, who he'd already started a journal on, seated herself across from him.

He couldn't remember, since he was so surprised, but Milton was fairly certain that he had let out a little squeak when their eyes met. This was a position he'd never been in. He wasn't exactly the type of guy that women like her made time to talk to.

She just stared at him for a few minutes, just staring and smiling. Was he supposed to say something? Even if he was, it was impossible. He could not talk to her now that she was a subject, and besides, his throat had gone completely dry. Other than the meek squeak, no words would come out.

Milton just stared right back until *she* finally spoke. It was the sweetest voice he'd ever heard, and sounded even sweeter up close, which made him even more hypnotized by this blonde beauty.

"There's no other reason you would be here this long, in this spot, unless you were watching me," she boldly said with a smile. Milton stared at her, blinking, helpless, flustered. He realized he had to say something.

"No. What? I, uh – Just what do you mean? Absurd. I'm simply, uh, reading this paper," he stammered at her.

"Oh really, then what's the front page story?"

He was caught. He knew it. Think fast, Milton told

himself.

"Well you see, uh, it isn't really the front page that I'm concerned with."

"Is that right," she cooed, making more of a statement than asking a question.

"Well yes it's right. I don't find interest in front page matters. It's the, uh, the buried stories that matter to me." He was finding his stride with this lie. "I'm a journalist. Any man can read the front, but what's interesting is what publishers are too scared to put up there," which was true.

Milton had always had an interest in what obscure things were going on in the world. And he felt that saying he was a journalist wasn't too far from the truth. After all, he researched things and wrote about them.

"That's very interesting Mr. —" she waited expectantly for him to introduce himself.

"Oh, uh, yes. Mr. Mentiro. Marcus Mentiro." He said, but he had no idea where the name came from. Maybe a story he'd been reading. Who knew.

"Mr. Mentiro," she said with a smile and extended her

hand to him, not to shake, but rather to kiss, which Milton found to be extremely odd and a bit presumptuous, though he happily kissed the top of her hand lightly, noticing how smooth she was. He made a mental note to write that down later.

She continued, "My name is Norma, and you still have to explain yourself Mr. Mentiro. Why are you watching me?"

He wasn't going to get out of this one. Best to just avoid the *whole* truth. That way it wasn't necessarily a lie. Milton took a deep breath and began.

"Well, to tell the truth Norma, I find you extremely attractive. In fact, you may be the most beautiful woman I have ever seen, and I just couldn't stop looking at you from the moment you sat down."

Milton was slowly beginning to realize that by actually talking to Norma, he could learn more about her than he had learned about anyone before. He could actually ask her about all of the people in her life, like the guy she was with.

Not only was Norma the most beautiful woman he'd ever seen, she could also be the one he knew the most about. His most thorough following yet.

"So tell me," Milton began, feeling more confident, now that he didn't have to be himself, "who was that man you were with before?"

He detected a slight hint of shyness on her part before she answered, "A gentleman caller, but he's a dullard if you couldn't tell," Norma said with a laugh.

Milton noticed her choice of words. She seemed to be fairly well-educated, or at least classically trained. This intrigued him.

"A gentleman caller huh? Well if that's all —" it was now or never, he told himself, fully realizing the magnanimous personal line he was about to cross, "I won't be stepping on any toes if I ask you to dinner then?"

Milton was feeling a sudden surge of confidence. It was easy for him to talk to Norma now that he was doing so as a part of his investigation, under the guise of an alter ego. This interaction had become a part of his constantly-forming plan, of which she knew nothing about.

"I'm free tomorrow night," she said with a glowing smile.

"Then so am I," Milton returned.

"Well Mr. Mentiro, I certainly am glad I came over here and had this chat with you. I'll meet you right here tomorrow night at seven," she said.

Milton had to remind himself not to get sucked into her tractor beam smile. "It's a date."

Norma walked away with a sway in her hips, knowing full well that Milton was looking, and he was.

He quickly pulled out his notebook and jotted some things down, but he wrote across the top of the cover: *WRITE VERY SMALL*.

~~~

Norma was proud of herself as she strode home. She didn't find Marcus particularly attractive, but she'd taken the risk of being deemed uninteresting and found that she was quite the opposite. By his standards anyway. Every man had different standards. She'd learned that as a child when nothing she did was impressive enough for her father. He never once told her he was proud of her. Not when she was the homecoming queen, or when she won the school's spelling bee. He'd attend everything she asked him to, but he never gave her any sense of approval.

This is why she liked the idea that Marcus really had stayed there to watch her the whole time she sat talking to another man. He was so enamored with her that he chose to stay while she was giving her time to someone else. This was just the confidence booster she needed heading into the audition tomorrow.

The problem was that Norma really didn't find the mousy man attractive. "Mr. Mentiro. What an odd name." she thought. But, you couldn't judge a man by his name, just like you can't judge a book by it's cover, or at least that's what she was told. But she always did the opposite.

If a book was covered in pink glitter, it could be about something horribly boring, like the history of baseball, but she'd buy it because it was so pretty! If there was a sexy, best-selling mystery novel in a plain brown cover, there was no way she'd pick it up.

Norma talked herself into realizing that Marcus Mentiro would be her greatest challenge yet. An unattractive man who was utterly infatuated with her. This was something she could deal with. It was the fact that his infatuation seemed somehow different from Guy being awestruck. It was the difference between being adored by someone and being impressive to them. Both of which she'd been searching for her whole life.

The walk home went quickly, as Norma's mind ran wild. Besides Marcus, she needed to practice for her audition tomorrow. It was for an ancillary part in a small theatrical production, but they'd already found someone to play the lead and the actress was related to some big wig producer. Norma knew that even if she only had a few lines, she'd be able to wow the man and hopefully finally get her big break. That's all she needed was someone to believe in her. For once.

Norma had been in the city for a few years, and was still waiting for something to happen. Every day she woke up, stretched her arms to the sky and thought about if today would be the day that her life turned into a real-life film.

Her thoughts involuntarily drifted back to Marcus and the date tomorrow. What would she wear? Norma had no idea where they were going, but she decided a cute, casual dress with high heels would do the trick. She'd lay it out when she got home.

Then it hit her. Maybe this *could be* Norma's complete movie. Maybe it was finally her turn! Here was this totally unassuming man who was clearly enamored with her; they'd had this great first encounter where she was witty and he played along, and now they were going out. Yes, maybe she'd finally walked right into her very own real-life movie romance. And if everything fell into place, she'd get the movie part too! Things were all starting to fall into place for her.

She'd have to rethink her outfit. If Norma had found her break in life, then she had to look amazing for it. Besides, if she dressed up, even if Marcus' plans were casual, he'd have to change them to accommodate what she was wearing.

Yes, she'd definitely wear something more formal.

This was all so exciting, Norma told herself as she slipped her key into the keyhole and turned the lock.

~~~

Milton was elated as he sped down the highway. He couldn't believe his luck! Here he was going on a date with a beautiful woman *and* he was going to get an insight into her life. He was going where he'd never gone before!

There was this feeling in his stomach. He felt a sick lightness. Like when you have a fever, only he wasn't sick. This was elation. The butterflies that he'd always heard about, but had always thought people were just generally full of shit when they talked about, the invisible insects were fluttering around.

Milton didn't think that he liked this feeling, and he

wanted it to go away, but at the same time he liked what was behind the feeling.

About halfway through his drive home, Milton realized that his cheeks hurt. He'd been stupidly smiling this whole time, and the revelation made him smile even bigger. He let out a little chuckle, which momentarily sobered him up. That was the first time he remembered audibly laughing in, well, years.

Milton's thoughts drifted to the last time he had laughed out loud. Occasionally he was amused, when children did funny things, or when someone fell, but he couldn't recall the last moment that he'd actually laughed for no reason.

This made Milton like the idea Norma even more. She had made him laugh, an out-loud laugh, and this revelation made Milton break into hysterics. He thought that he must look crazy to anyone who saw him, but he didn't care.

It was the first time Milton had felt happiness in a very long time, and he was loathe to lose it.

~~~

Norma was getting ready for her big date, and had already changed outfits several times. The rejected ones lay strewn about her floor, and she currently wore a tight fitting red dress with a slightly flared skirt.

This was appropriate for most outings, Norma decided. Tight enough to be sexy, but flouncy enough for a casual lunch, when paired with the right shoes or course. Her hair was perfectly curled, and she wore bright red lips. She loved bright red lips because they were striking and she also felt they would deter a man from kissing her, because she loved turning a man down on a first date; she felt that it proved instantly to the man that she's not that kind of girl, or at least that was what she would tell herself.

Norma left her apartment and waited at the coffee shop where the duo had first met, but there was no sign of Marcus, which began to worry her. She was already 30 minutes late, because she liked to draw attention while making an entrance. It also gave her something to immediately talk about, explaining what had kept her so long, but maybe that had been the wrong move with this odd man. Norma was used to men waiting around for her, eager for their date, but what if Marcus was different? What if he wasn't that infatuated with her and had left? After all, *she'd* been the one who approached *him*. Or, what if he was like her and he'd simply trumped her lateness.

Norma was amused at the idea and took a seat at one

of the tables, waiting for her date. She sat up very straight, making sure her perky breasts were pressed upward in her tight bodice. She lightly fluffed her hair, ensuring that it looked perfect, then scanned her surroundings. Last, but not least, she took out a compact to check her makeup.

"If he doesn't come soon," she thought to herself, "then I'm going to leave. I can't be seen waiting around like this!"

Just as Norma snapped her compact closed, Marcus was standing right there in front of her, as if he'd just appeared out of nowhere, and it startled her. She tried to laugh it off, but truly wondered where in the world he had popped up from. He didn't give an explanation about why he was late, but just extended a hand and off they went.

~~~

Milton had in fact arrived 30 minutes early for the date and found himself a desirable hiding place in the bushes so he could watch Norma arrive. He needed to notate things like the way the subject walked, the amount of confidence she had, what she was wearing.

As their agreed upon time passed, Milton began to wonder if he'd been stood up, but then he thought back to Mother who was always late to everything. She found it important to make an entrance, and Milton postulated that Norma may be the same way. So he continued to wait.

But as time wore on, he began to wonder if he'd been stupid to not follow her home initially. What if she didn't show? He'd already started a journal on her and he couldn't very well just stop it because he'd lost track of her. No, that would be a disgrace. He thought for a moment that he may have to spend the rest of his life tracking down this blonde woman, "which is actually bit romantic in a twisted sort of way," he thought to himself. This wasn't about romance though!

Milton was on a focused mission to observe someone more completely than he thought was possible. That's what he needed to keep reminding himself.

As the minutes ticked by, Milton became more nervous that the subject wouldn't show. He saw people coming and going, but still no Norma. He contemplated leaving after she was 30 minutes late, but where would he go? Sitting outside this cafe was his best shot at finding her again, so he decided to stay, even if it took all night.

Just as Milton started getting antsy, Norma showed. In a bright red dress that hugged her every curve, she sashayed to the cafe, looking around for her date. Him! He was almost in shock at the realization that she was here, dressed like that, for *him*!

So, Milton made a few notes as she sat down, nervously primping herself.

Seems anxious and surprised. After sitting down, acts a bit insecure about being alone. Smiles back at people who catch her eye.

When choosing this hiding spot, Milton realized he'd made one crucial mistake. He hadn't considered how he'd make his exit unseen by Norma. He began to panic, because he'd look rather silly stepping out of a large bush and walking to the table, but with a stroke of luck, she pulled out a compact, and while she was engrossed with herself, Milton made his move. He confidently walked up to Norma and waited until she saw him standing across from her.

As she snapped her compact shut, Norma spotted him, and she jumped. He'd startled her, which he liked in an odd way. She smiled at him and said, "Well Mr. Mentiro, I never thought I'd meet a man who liked to be later than I do.

He laughed and apologized, but of course he couldn't tell her what he'd been doing; so he just offered to help her up, then extended his arm. "Shall we?" he said.

And they were off on their first date of many.

~~~

Their most memorable date happened by accident.

Norma had been window shopping, because it had been awhile since she'd gotten a gig. But she read somewhere that buying one thing a week increased a person's lifespan by five years. So, she made it a point to buy at least one nice thing for herself a week, even if it meant going without food for a day or so.

It was a sunny day, but not too hot, and Norma was commanding the attention of everyone on the sidewalk with her swaying hips that filled out her rose colored dress perfectly. She stopped at each window, carefully inspecting what they had to offer. Then she happened upon a store with a bright red SALE poster, beaming at her like a sign from God.

Once Norma walked into the vacant store, she was swarmed by salespeople, like she was chum in a sea of sharks. Loving the attention, she was caught up in the moment and let them show her shoes, dresses, and handbags – all of which were full price, of course –

before she sweetly broke them the bad news.

It was too embarrassing for Norma to admit that she was broke, and instead just said she was buying a gift for a friend, and it needed to be inexpensive because she didn't want the friend to feel uncomfortable. Crestfallen, the salespeople waved her over to a corner in the back that was hidden so well she might not have found it without their direction.

Norma walked back there, perusing as she went, and took a look at what she could afford. A small silk scarf was $70 and there were three leather coin purses that were $120 each. If she only spent $70, then she'd have money leftover to eat at the bistro down the street, but no one could tell what designer it was just from a silly scarf. She'd have to tell everyone, and it always sounded pathetic when people did that. At least the coin purse was recognizable with the designer's logo emblazoned throughout the leather. But she had nothing left to do for the day, and figured she'd need a scarf at some point in her life.

Picking a bright yellow and orange pattern that matched her dress, Norma walked up to the cashier. She handed him a $100 bill, and walked out. She didn't have $100 bills on her often, but her money wasn't usually very pretty. A few folded and unorganized $20s, folded around a couple of dingy $1s, and a $5 bill that had been taped back together by it's previous owner. This meant that she needed to take a trip to the bank before every shopping trip. If she couldn't be rich, she could at least seem like she was with her crisp bills.

After leaving the store, Norma took out the scarf, rolled it up, and tied it around her neck, like a neckerchief, but she still carried the empty shopping bag because it felt fancier. When she got to the little bistro, it was busy, and there was only one table, directly in the sun. It wasn't ideal, but Norma was starving, and she'd given up the coin purse that everyone would notice so that she could have a latte and biscotti.

Agreeing to take the table, Norma sat right in the sun, while everyone around her huddled under their umbrellas. She hadn't thought it was that hot out until this moment, when she was sure it was nearing 100 degrees.

The waiter walked over to her, and just as Norma was about to order, she caught a glimpse of Marcus walking past the gate. "Marcus!" she called out to him, still sitting, but completely ignoring her server. "MARCUS!" she yelled louder, half-standing this time. The man still didn't look, but Norma was positive it was him. She got up and walked over to the fence. Right when he strolled next to her, she reached out and touched his arm.

"Marcus!" Norma sternly, but happily said a final time. "What are you doing here?" She thought he looked surprised, and not as excited as she'd hoped.

"Oh, h-hi," he stammered.

~~~

Milton hated few things more than he hated when Norma would go shopping. He was used to sitting in bushes, and doing that type of thing, but there was nothing as boring, or more challenging than following and observing a shopper. Stores were only so big so he couldn't follow her inside, or she'd see him. Even if he could follow her inside, she was easy to lose once she entered the dressing rooms.

This meant Milton had to creep around, keeping both an eye on Norma, and on the stores that she went into. To do this, he'd stand far, far away; so far down the street that there was no way Norma would even think to look his way, but in her salmon dress, it was hard to lose track of her.

Today, Norma only stopped in one store, which was very good news for Milton, but he couldn't help feeling sad for this woman whom he loved so much. It was obvious how much Norma liked new and expensive things, and while Milton could afford them, he was very careful with his money, considering he needed it to last forever. Which meant he rarely got Norma expensive presents, and she seemed okay enough with it.

But when Norma disappeared into the store having a sale, Milton knew he had to find a way to help her salvage her day, because something about having to buy things on sale just sucked a little joy out of the entire experience.

This particular store was a little more tricky than others. Milton walked by the window several times, eventually deciding that it might not be too risky to go inside. So, Milton went in the front door and started looking at something on the opposite side of the store from Norma.

But things started to go wrong when the flock of salespeople who had been helping Norma all came running over to him once she was done with them. Milton was overwhelmed and quickly left the store before he could be noticed, but he'd seen Norma glance his way, and he wasn't positive that he hadn't been spotted.

There was no time to look back for confirmation, and Milton scurried to the corner of the street to watch from afar until Norma decided to leave. Sometimes she stayed for a very long time, and others just a little while, but there was really no way to be sure. However, Milton had already picked up on some of Norma's little idiosyncrasies, and he liked to try and guess what she'd do next.

So far today, Norma had seemed like she wasn't in the best of moods, which usually led to her shopping for a shorter amount of time because nothing could really amuse her for very long when she was in a mood like this one. She had to keep her mind occupied so that she wouldn't have time to get sad. This meant that Milton gave her about five more minutes before he saw her step out of the store, based on how long she'd already been in there.

While he waited, Milton watched the people around him passing him by. Few even noticed a person was there; he was more of an obstacle in the way of their walking path. Over the time he'd been observing people, it was becoming more and more common for people to stare at their phones while they walked, or to have their headphones on. Anything to make them feel like they were in their own little bubble, and not surrounded by millions of people. Really, the only people who talked to strangers anymore were homeless people and drug addicts.

After a few minutes had gone by, Milton noticed Norma leaving the store and mentally patted himself on the back. From the time on his watch, it had been four minutes and 30 seconds until Norma had emerged, and he quickly noted it in the journal before scurrying off after her.

Milton watched as Norma took a brightly colored scarf from her bag and carefully tied it around her neck. It made her look a little washed out, but the colors fit her personality. Warm, bubbly, eye-catching. As he walked and wrote in his journal, Milton realized he was joining the throngs of people walking around in their own world, only he was in two at once.

Just like when he guessed how long it would be until Norma left the store, Milton also tried to guess where she'd be off to next. This time, he was guessing she'd want to grab something to eat. It was a warm day, and she had a new accessory to show off. A restaurant with a patio was the perfect place for such an occasion.

Sure enough, Milton watched as Norma entered one of the most overpriced bistros in the city, then emerged in the middle of the patio. From where he was standing, it would be hard to see her, because too many loud people were in the way. So, he took a deep breath and walked past the patio, aiming to get to the other side where it was quieter and where there were less people since it was directly in the sun. He tried to look straight ahead, and prayed that she didn't spot him.

But then he heard it; the most terrifying and wonderful sound in the world: Norma calling his fake name.

"Oh, h-hi," he stammered.

"Marcus, what are you doing here!?" she happily exclaimed.

"I was just on my way home from an appointment. With a source I'm interviewing for a new book," he hurriedly added.

"Well that's great luck! Come join me. You're just in time for lunch."

Milton knew that his hidden research for the day was done, and that wasn't the worst thing in the world. It was hard to follow Norma around all of the time and not be able to tell her things, to hold her hand, to kiss her for no reason. And besides, this was when the *real* secret research began anyway. He walked inside, sat down at the table across from Norma, and fell in love all over again. However, "I like your scarf. Is it new?" is all that he could manage to say.

She went on and on about the scarf, making the purchasing process sound much more glamorous than it actually was, since Milton had seen much of the entire transaction happen. But it was one of the things he loved about Norma. She had a way of turning the most mundane thing into something magical.

Milton sat there, half listening, half thinking about where they'd be off to next, because there always had to be *somewhere* they went to next. This would also give Norma lots of chances to show off her new scarf too, which he knew she would love. So, when the bill came, Milton looked to Norma, with her big, hopeful eyes and asked if she wanted to go to the park.

"That's sounds like a fantastic idea! Let's do it!," she emphatically said.

Milton left cash for the server – Norma didn't even reach for her wallet, she never did – and headed out, arm-in-arm.

~~~

"The park! This will be fun!" Norma thought to herself. It wasn't the most exciting thing she could think of, but it wasn't a terrible idea either. She loved being around people when she was looking and feeling great. Everyone stared at her, and that was when she felt most in her element. It was always hard for Norma to understand why some people wanted to live their whole lives going unnoticed. It didn't seem to make any sense!

People bought cute clothes, they went to the gym to work out, and yet for some reason, they wanted to go through life without anyone noticing. That sounded like a miserable existence, and Norma wanted no part of it.

That's another thing she was loving about Marcus was how much freedom he gave her to be herself, including giving her the attention she craved.

Though, she wished she'd have known she wouldn't have had to pay for lunch because she would have bought something more expensive at the store. "Not that there was anything more alluring and versatile than this scarf anyway," Norma told herself to feel better.

Marcus paid the check – Norma didn't believe in paying for things when she was in the company of a man. He should have thought of that before asking her out – and they left the bistro, with everyone staring. She reveled in the attention that her odd looking relationship garnered. While she considered herself to be fairly humble, it wasn't lost on Norma that she was completely out of Marcus' league, which made people mumble to each other as they walked past. If only he could wear a shirt that said 'Rich Man' it would all make sense.

But she didn't care one way or the other. People were looking and she was wearing a fabulous new scarf that was making them all jealous, and she was on the arm of a person who adored her.

~~~

Norma's young adult life was anything but normal, and she rarely liked to talk about it.

After leaving home at 17, without finishing High School, she was pretty lost for awhile, working whatever jobs she could find, whether it was a sales clerk at a store so cheap they called it Hi Fashion, or whether she was a waitress in one of the worst parts of town. She made it work.

Along the way, she'd met the only person she'd ever loved more than Marcus, and that was Adam. Never in a million years did Norma think she'd fall for a poor cashier, and she couldn't explain why she had, but it was the deepest love she'd ever felt for someone.

Things were just different this time.

Adam was a salesperson at Hi Fashion, and he was 17 years Norma's senior, which Norma found out was 35 years old after she consulted her calculator. But that didn't matter. Adam had a young soul, and was always goofing around, telling Norma things about life that she'd never thought of before.

It was the first time in her life that someone treated Norma like an equal, and not just some pretty young thing to stare at and talk about, but would never directly talk to her.

And while Norma knew she was in the prime of her good looks, she also knew that Adam didn't look his age at all. He had a youthful face, and shaggy jet-black hair that he sometimes put in a ponytail. He wore a watch to work that beeped every hour, on the hour, and he had a swimmers body, because every morning, he'd swim 2 miles before even having breakfast.

Norma knew that they'd built a friendship over the few weeks she'd worked there, but she never thought that it was heading anywhere romantically, until it did. One day, they grabbed a drink after work, like they usually did, and after one too many, Adam leaned over and kissed Norma lightly on the lips.

It didn't feel wrong, so she let it happen. After that night, the couple was inseparable, and even though Adam wasn't necessarily obsessed with Norma, she got all of the attention and love that she needed. They'd talk about their futures, share hair products, eat just frosting out of the container at night because it was what they felt like doing.

Soon, they were living together, until tragedy struck.

Norma was always secretly waiting for the hammer to drop; it didn't feel right for her to be this happy all of the time. She'd spent her whole life unhappily looking for happiness, and now that she'd found it, the thought of losing it was too hard. It seemed like no one else in the world woke up every morning with a smile on their face, so why should it be okay for her to.

And one night, when she was sitting at home, waiting for Adam to close up the store, she got a knock at the door. Two men from the coroner's office were there to tell Norma that Adam had been in a car accident, and had died on impact. It took a few moments for the news to sink in, as she stared at the strangers standing in her doorway. It felt wrong for them to be there. They didn't know Norma and they didn't know Adam, so why were these people here for this moment?

It didn't matter. Norma melted into the couch right where she'd been sitting before. She felt sad, but not totally surprised. She made it a point to constantly be ready for any sad situation to strike. True happiness was always an ideal situation, not a reality, and real life could happen at any moment. This was real life.

The men asked if she needed anything, and she said no, waving them to the door, letting the silent tears fall.

Norma never told anyone about Adam after that. No one wants to think about something perfect that they possessed for only a brief moment. It was always more painful than helpful. So, over the years, Norma buried Adam.

~~~

Several months passed and Norma had fallen head over heels in love with Marcus. The kind of love where her thoughts were consumed by him, and she thought of all her future plans with him in mind. When they kissed, she got butterflies, every single time. But she couldn't figure out if he felt the same way, and she was apprehensive about expressing what she was feeling.

He was a very quiet man, Mr. Mentiro, and Norma couldn't always tell what he was thinking. Sometimes she thought she saw love in his eyes, others she felt like he was studying her, as though she were a science project and he was visually dissecting her, watching her every move. She couldn't figure him out, and it made her uneasy.

Tonight, they were going to see a movie in the park and have a picnic dinner. They'd talked about doing this for some time now, but they had finally decided on a movie both of them wanted to see, though Marcus had agreed to nearly every option she'd proposed.

Norma had a burning question for Marcus, and she couldn't handle it any longer. Tonight she had to ask him. It was something she'd thought long and hard about over the months that they had been dating. The more she was around this guy the more she liked him.

It seemed about time to ask him to move in together. She wasn't sure if he'd want to live in her little apartment, but he'd never asked her over to his home, so that made her cautious as well. Her hope was that he'd say yes, and they'd get a little place together where they could start to build a life.

Of course, Norma was nervous about what Marcus would say, but he seemed like a traditional guy, so if she wanted him to do anything nontraditional, she was going to have to be the one to ask him.

Surely it wouldn't be that way when they got married, because Norma knew Marcus would want to be the man of the house and to take care of her. As soon as she showed him her confidence in him, then Marcus would be much more forward than he is now. But moving in together was something she'd have to put on the table.

Norma had always found it odd that they always went to her apartment and never to his home. When she asked about it, Marcus claimed that it was very far away. Too far out of the way, really, and that it was terribly uninviting. That's why he spent all day out in the city.

"Well why don't you move somewhere new?" Norma had once asked him.

"This house has been in my family for generations and I couldn't bear to get rid of it. There are just too many memories there," Marcus answered, then tried to change the subject.

She still found these explanations odd, but Norma respected Marcus's wishes for her not to go there. She knew what it was like to be ashamed of living somewhere.

When Norma moved to the city, her first apartment had been so awful that she hardly had any friends at all for fear that they would want to come over and hang out. The self- ostracization was more than she could handle and she moved before her year-long lease was up. Of course, she was able to talk the landlord out of making her pay a fee for the early termination.

Even as a child, Norma was ashamed of the run-down trailer that she lived in with her mom and dad. She was an only child, and her mom was constantly working double shifts at the diner, while her dad took care of her during the day. At night, he'd go to the local dump where he was the graveyard-shift security guy. From a young age it wasn't unusual for Norma to fall asleep on her pull-out sofa bed with no one home except herself. She couldn't understand how her parents worked so hard, yet never were able to afford a nicer place to live. But their home was the least of her worries growing up.

Now, as a semi-successful adult, Norma was in a beautiful one bedroom apartment that overlooked the city, and she wanted Milton to join her. She wanted him to be a part of her world every day.

~~~

Milton found himself falling deeper and deeper in love with Norma daily. He struggled to take unbiased notes about her, sometimes finding it to be nearly impossible! When she did something boneheaded, Milton would jot down tiny justifications for things because he struggled to be critical of her. It would end up looking messy with his scribbles; he hated scribbles and berated himself for these lapses in judgment.

Watches soap operas in the middle of the day while

eating out of a gallon carton of ice cream. Mint chip.
~~She had a hard week, so she deserved this.~~

But Milton didn't care. He just loved Norma and wanted to be with her as much as possible, but he knew, as each day came to a close, that he was one page closer to ending his relationship with her. Just the thought of it was hard to bear, so when it crept into his mind, Milton pushed it far, far away. He even took extra care to write his notes as small as possible, while still ensuring that they were legible, since he knew that he would reread *this particular* journal later. He wanted to make every word count. It wasn't often that Milton re-read his journals – in fact, he'd only done it once before – but this was a different circumstance than previous encounters.

~~~

Milton had once observed a woman so sad, that she ended up killing herself. A few weeks after he'd completed her journal, Milton saw the woman's picture in the newspaper. He recognized her immediately, and couldn't believe that she'd gone through with it.

During the entire time he'd followed Diane, she exhibited all of the classic signs of being depressed and lonely. Some days she couldn't get out of bed – which were the days when Milton wrote in large print to take up room because he was so bored – and every night she'd drink herself to sleep. In fact, during the whole time he followed her, Diane never met up with a friend or took a phone call that wasn't about work. She seemed as alone as a person can get.

Sure enough, in the article, it said that her landlord found her two weeks after she'd died, the coroner confirmed. She'd asked for the time off from work, and in her suicide note she left before hanging herself, Diane wrote:
"Make sure everyone knows how long I've been dead; how long it took them to find me. That's how alone I am..."

Those words haunted Milton, and he felt compelled to re-read the journal, to try and cope with this bizarre loss. No matter how hard he tried not to, Milton still occasionally felt attached to his subjects. They were people he had come to know intimately, and while he felt no actual emotion toward them, he felt an intense empathy. The entire time he'd followed Diane, he'd wanted to reach out, to let her know that she wasn't alone, but that wasn't an option. Now, here he was, trying to figure out how he could have helped, but nothing came to mind.

~~~

One night, after they had been drinking at her place, Norma asked about Milton's family. What they were like, did he have any brothers or sisters, were his parents still alive.

Normally, Milton talked about his family as little as possible, but tonight, Milton had had enough to drink, and was feeling particularly twitterpated, so he let it slip that his mother had left him a fairly large sum of money when she died. Though, he left out the details of the mental hospital and how he ended up there.

"Why don't you ever talk about your family?" Norma started.

"Well, you don't talk about yours very much either, dear."

"That's fair. But I want to hear about how *you* grew up. *I* already know how *I* grew up." She paused. "Things like what your house was like. You said it's where you live now, but since I can't go there, you simply must tell me about it!" Norma exclaimed.

Taken up in her excitement, and feeling loose-lipped, Milton started talking about the house. Before he knew it, he'd said, "When my mother died, she left me all of her money."

It was both the phrasing and the message that made Norma's eyes light up, and Milton knew it. She'd lit up like the Fourth of July, and he knew that she was never going to leave him now. He'd never know if this gorgeous woman really loved *him*, or if it was the money she was after.

This was a thought Milton both loved and loathed. Normally, he wouldn't care if a woman was interested in him for his money, but Norma was different. He wanted her to love him for him. Well, the *him* that she knew. Marcus. But was Marcus that different from Milton?

Aside from the journals, Milton and Marcus were very similar. Their main difference being that Marcus was more confident than mousy Milton. And, of course, that Norma didn't know who Milton was at all.

The couple had been together for awhile now, and Milton was feeling torn. Over that six months, he had grown closer to Norma than he had to anyone in his life. Except for Jenny, because she knew things about Milton that he was too nervous to tell Norma. However, Norma was the only person who engaged with Milton, whereas Jenny sat there, staring straight ahead.

While they were together, Milton told himself that he was acting as Marcus, so it wasn't that big of a deal to leave out some less savory parts of his life. At times, Milton could really convince himself that he was someone else, and that certain things never happened to him.

But because Milton was this different person, this *Marcus*, he didn't feel like he had to tell Norma about things like killing the pool boy, the mental hospital, and the soccer coach. Those were things that happened to Milton, not Marcus. Similarly, Milton realized that his compulsions were his own as well, so Marcus didn't need to concern himself with them. Though, Milton was constantly taking mental notes while pretending to be Marcus. It was all so complex and contradictory, but it somehow made sense in his mind.

About three months in, Milton realized that he was following the woman he wanted to marry, but he didn't know what to do about the damn journals! He couldn't give them up entirely, but surely his bride-to-be would wonder where he went all day once Milton had to move on from her to another subject.

The couple spent a considerable amount of time together, and the reason they were able to was because it was all research for Milton, and he frequently crossed her path. However, once he had a new woman in his life – since he would never follow another man again after being so greatly disappointed – he would spend much less time with Norma, and he knew she would not like that at all.

That was part of what Milton loved so much about Norma: her intense need for attention. He loved it because Milton was able to give this lonely girl what she wanted, and he got to see the look of satisfaction on her face when he doted on her. It was so endearing how she loved that Milton noticeably watched her every move.

It really seemed like Norma loved being watched by him, which helped ease some of his guilt while following her around. He was pretty sure any of his other subjects would have called the police on him if they'd seen him hanging around one too many times. Though, he wasn't positive Norma wouldn't do the same if she ever found out.

If this relationship was going to work, Milton had to start tapering off his time spent with Norma as Marcus, and spend more time as Milton. He knew that he risked losing her to someone who focused on her 24-7, but he had to if he wanted to be with her long after the journal was over.

And Milton would still be spending just as much time as usual with Norma, only in secret. She wouldn't know, and that was the catch.

Slowly, Milton started finding more and more excuses as to why they couldn't see each other. He had a meeting, or some work was being done on his house.

He painfully rebuffed Norma's attempts to squeeze herself into his schedule.

And he could feel Norma slowly pulling away...

~~~

Norma just couldn't understand it. What could she possibly have done that would have made Marcus spend so much less time with her. They went from spending nearly every waking moment together, to dates a few times a week, and a sleepover here and there. She found herself daydreaming about him, growing sad about his absence. More than his absence, she was sad because of the lack of attention she was getting.

Drinking wine daily had become a habit for Norma. She wanted hard alcohol, but wine seemed more ladylike and glamorous; she drank white wine during the day, and red at night. Of course, she wasn't exactly sure that's what glamorous people did, but whenever she was at a fancy restaurant, she'd noticed most of the women ordered wine, or water with a wedge of lemon, but water just wasn't going to cut it right now.

When Marcus wasn't around, Norma tried to do everything to take her mind off of him, but it didn't work. She found herself seeing him everywhere that she went.

At her audition the day before, Norma could have sworn she saw Marcus driving his car just a few vehicles behind her. Her heart leapt, and she thought maybe he was coming to surprise and support her. As Norma pulled up to the building, she noticed the car was gone and her heart sank.

Norma sat in the front seat, holding her emotions at bay, because this particular audition was for the part of a blonde bimbo, which she couldn't do very successfully if she was a crying mess. She channeled the bubbliest, happiest person she could be, but it wasn't enough.

It was the worst audition Norma had ever had.

Today though, Norma decided to go to the Farmers Market to get her mind off Marcus... and to try and be discovered. She could have sworn that she saw his face in the crowd at least a dozen times, but every time she did a double take, he vanished. She was so sure she had seen him though!

Norma had decided that if Marcus couldn't give her the time and love that she needed, as well as the attention she craved, then she would just have to find someone else who could. She would have to break up with him for good. As sad as it made her, it was what had to be done.

Foregoing a glass for the bottle, Norma sat on her couch, drinking wine, and thinking about how she would break up with Marcus.

Then Norma remembered the money.

How much money was it exactly? She needed to find out if it was enough to keep her happy for the rest of her life. If not, then she was definitely gone.

~~~

One afternoon when Norma was about six years old, her mother had only been able to pick up the morning shift at the diner, which meant that she was home at the same time as Norma's father, and that almost always meant trouble. Norma was never sure how they always had so much to fight about, but they did, and one time it ended up with her mother being rushed to the emergency room.

Her mother came in from work, grabbed the bottle of gin that was hidden on top of the cupboard, and poured herself a glass. Norma never understood why her mother didn't just keep the bottle *in* the cupboard, but it was always best to ask as little questions as she needed to.

Just as her mother finished gulping her glass, Norma's father walked out of the bedroom and into the kitchen. He stared at her mother with his steely, expressionless eyes, and Norma felt a tension. She was waiting for the words to fly, but her father just brushed past his wife, grabbed his coat and walked out the front door.

Both Norma and her mother exhaled a sigh of relief, not even realizing they'd been holding their breath until now. There would be no fighting today, and that meant it was a very good day.

~~~

This was proving to be increasingly more complicated than Milton had anticipated. Norma had become angry and irritable, and more vulnerable than Milton liked a woman to be, frankly.

Milton fell in love with the *confident* Norma who knew all eyes were on her and LOVED it; not this sad Norma who was begging for his affection.

And she'd been bringing up his money a lot lately. Much more than made him comfortable.

It unnerved Milton because it only made him more positive that Norma was just after him for his wealth. He knew he wasn't the best looking guy in town, but he still thought he deserved more than a person who only loved him for his wealth.

Norma wanted to know how exactly much he was worth, if it was locked up in a trust fund, or if it was an inheritance that was left to him. It seemed like his fortune was every third topic that she talked about.

So Milton lied. He said it was a small fortune, left as an inheritance, and he was worth roughly $1 million, which wasn't enough for life, so he had to work very hard at investments and building his wealth. That's how he spent his free time, his time away from her; as far as she knew anyway.

Milton hated lying to Norma, but it was clear that about some topics, white lies were necessary.

~~~

It wasn't quite as much as she was hoping for, but Norma was happy with that amount, or at least she felt she could be. "And Marcus said he was doing things to stretch the money, so I can definitely be comfortable," she thought to herself.

After debating it in her mind, over a bottle of wine, Norma decided that she could withstand Marcus's inattention as long as she was going to have a comfortable future. Knowing what she knew, it was certain that he could provide for her, and he seemed to want to.

As the weeks wore on, Norma was passed over for several acting parts, and she became depressed. A bottle of wine a day turned into two, then three, then so many that she stopped counting. Her face started puffing up and she looked bloated. But she'd rather give up food than the lovely bottle.

So, Norma suggested that she and Marcus start going to lounges rather than restaurants. At a lounge she would be expected to drink, and wouldn't feel pressured to eat. When Marcus wasn't around, she'd try to bide her time by practicing for upcoming auditions and scanning the newspaper and local magazines for open calls.

None of this seemed to curb Norma's insatiable need for attention though. She craved Marcus's gaze, staring blatantly at her. Like he was watching her every move, and storing it away in his memory, presumably to replay during those times when she wasn't around.

Or at least that's what Norma told herself. She began to think again about what a life would be like without Marcus. She could date, and enjoy the adoration of as many men as she wanted. They would call her and take her out on grand dates.

The main problem came down the the fact that Norma didn't want another man. She'd been on lots of dates with other men, and they were all lacking something; time, money, conversation. Norma wanted Marcus. He was the ultimate key to her happiness, and without him around, she was bitterly depressed.

~~~

It was heartbreaking for Milton to watch the woman he loved fall into such depths of sadness on his account. He wrestled with himself. Was it selfish to leave Norma alone for so long and study her from outside the house where she couldn't see him?

Milton decided it was entirely necessary for his purposes. He was gathering invaluable information about Norma and about what made her tick. In fact, if he hadn't fallen in love with her, he likely would have detested her lack of self-worth, and her extreme neediness. She was co-dependent and insecure, which were all turnoffs for Milton. But since he was in love, he adored her for these things. He also found it odd that he was starting to exhibit many of the behaviors he'd wondered about his subjects for years.

As the outsider, it was easy to objectively make observations about people, like if they were actually funny, or if they were a socially inept person. However, in his observations, Milton found that even people's most undesirable traits somehow seemed invisible to the people who loved them. And once they came to light, the relationships frequently fizzled. He hoped that wasn't what would happen here.

It was hard work following Norma around without her noticing. Milton was sure she had spotted him a few times, but since she never brought it up, he assumed he was wrong.

When Milton picked Norma up to go out, he'd ask her how her day was, knowing full well what she'd been doing the whole time. He found it adorable how she embellished the simplest story. Like when she overtly explained the quaintness of the Farmers Market, and how all the booth owners had flirted with her, but she told them firmly that she was taken, and very deeply in love.

Milton knew that Norma hadn't stopped and talked at a single booth and had bought nothing, but he played along with her stories because he loved her smile and the way her mouth moved when she talked.

Sometimes, if Milton was feeling particularly brave, he'd ask Norma leading questions about things she hadn't mentioned. Like one time she spilled coffee on her blouse right as she was leaving the apartment building to meet him for lunch. She clearly felt clumsy, looking up and down the street to see if anyone had noticed, before skittering inside to change her top. So, when they sat down for lunch, Milton asked, "Don't you just hate it when you spill things on yourself?" and waited to see her reaction.

Norma blushed slightly, and with the words caught in her throat finally said, "How did you –" But Milton cut her off explaining, "I had to change this shirt right before I left because I spilled coffee all over it. That's why I was a little late." It opened Norma up. Her smile softened and she quietly proclaimed, "That exact same thing happened to me!"

Occasionally, Norma would ask how Milton's day was, but he'd learned that he could shrug out an answer and she'd move on, knowing herself that she was the more interesting of the two. Also, if Milton had even tried to explain financial things to her, they both knew it would be more effort than it was worth.

When they were together, Milton would never have had a thought that she was so miserable without him, which is why he was so shocked at what would happen after he'd drop her off and leave.

Each time, Norma would sit on her bed and sob uncontrollably, while looking at a picture of the two of them together. It hurt Milton so badly to see her in this state, as he peered through the window from his hiding place, and a few times he'd come dangerously close to rapping on the window, revealing his hiding spot, and telling her about everything, but he knew that could only end badly.

So, Milton jotted down his tiny notes, occasionally staining the pages with his own tears, causing the ink to run. When that happened, it made Milton so irritated with himself that he snapped right out of his sadness, scolding himself for the mistake.

Then one night it happened. The conversation Milton had been dreading, but knew would eventually come. The next time they were together, Norma brought up the topic of marriage and by the look on her face it was clear that she was dead serious. She asked Milton if he wanted a life with her, and why he had never discussed it, since it was the next obvious step in their relationship.

Knowing that someday this question would come, Milton had an answer prepared, explaining to Norma that he was just very busy right now. "Of course I see a future with you!" Milton said with a meager smile before continuing, "Just not marriage in the immediate future."

~~~

This answer was unsatisfactory for Norma, and she was shocked that Marcus would even try to sell her this load of crap. Either she was good enough for him to be with, or she wasn't. Plain and simple.

After this, Norma felt that Milton needed to be punished, so she caused a scene in the restaurant. She yelled and screamed about how awful he was to her, how he never *really* loved her and how she could have any man she wanted. But she'd chosen him and obviously he didn't give a damn.

~~~

Milton tried to throw in his two cents, but it was no use. Right now, she was acting out the role of 'Enraged and Indignant Norma,' to a room full of restaurant goers, and while the underlying feelings were sincere, she was still loving the attention more than anything.

The fight ended as Milton had expected, with Norma storming out of the restaurant, hailing a cab and heading home.

Milton hurriedly paid the bill. He had to see what kind of further reaction Norma would have, despite how badly he was hurting emotionally right now. The journals always came first. He assumed the actress' private reaction would be a smug one. Proud of herself for her overall performance.

But as Milton crept into his hiding place underneath Norma's window, he could hear her shuffling around slamming drawers and cursing through her tears.

Pulling out his journal, Milton began to feverishly take notes, while struggling to avoid the light cascading from her window into the alley. Then he heard Norma saying that if he didn't want to be with her, she should just end the relationship altogether.

Norma was no longer crying, but sounded eerily focused. Milton studied what she was pulling from the drawers. Razors.

~~~

Norma sat down on her bed, and looked at the razor as she bared her wrist. The bottle of wine was calling to her, so she briefly looked away from the shining blade, and took a swig of the Merlot. It was a cheap wine that she'd bought earlier that day. Killing herself hadn't been a part of her schedule when Norma had chosen the drink, otherwise she would have picked something much better than this $10 red. "It's good for the money, though," Norma told herself as she took a few gulps.

Dying with nothing but a bottle of cheap wine in her stomach seemed almost poetic to Norma. She'd died struggling for love, and for the art of acting.

"Her greatest role was her demise," was what Norma hoped someone wrote about her in the newspaper obituary. Or something along those lines anyway. It had to be something grand, that conveyed how tragic her loss was for the world.

Unfortunately, deep down inside, Norma knew that she wasn't a movie star. If she died here in this tub, no one would pay attention. In fact, if she hadn't been mostly convinced that Marcus was following her, then who knows how long it would be until someone came along and smelled something coming from her apartment.

No, Norma couldn't have her rotting stench be what drew people here. That was an awful legacy to leave behind. Even so, she was struggling to pull the blade away from her porcelain skin.

If Marcus was watching from somewhere, she wanted him to remember this as her greatest performance. She cried out, "We'll see how much he wants to be with me when I'm gone."

Then she heard it –

~~~

Milton looked panicked. Norma wouldn't really do it would she? If she did would he interfere? She'd know all about the fact that he was following her if he did, and his cover would be completely blown. If the poor girl reacted badly, then she could call the police on Milton, and then he'd be locked up, again.

This was the woman he loved though! Milton couldn't just stand by and watch all of this happen! That was ludicrous!

Norma got distracted and took a drink of wine, then a long gulp. "Good, she's talking some sense into herself. If she's distracted, she won't be able to do it," Milton thought to himself. But as he said it, Norma put the blade back near her wrist.

Milton was very worried now, and Norma said, "We'll see how much he wants to be with me when I'm gone."

As Norma touched the blade to her wrist, Milton squeaked out, "No!"

~~~

"What the hell? Norma thought," as she jumped, pulling the blade away from her. She looked to her window and saw the shape of a head duck down out of the corner of her eye. She ran over and saw Marcus cowering below her windowsill.

"Marcus?" Norma said in bewilderment, as she looked down at the meek little man. She couldn't hide the slight hint of happiness in her voice at the sight of him. She hadn't been crazy after all.

Marcus stood up as tall as he could, which was still a small stature compared to the average man. He was holding a tattered, grubby journal in his hands and looked incredibly guilty.

"I couldn't – I was just – You were – I – I just couldn't let you do it!" he said, almost ashamedly.

She was trying to get a grip on the situation.

"Why were you under my window?"

"I – Well, it's complicated. Can I come in?"

Marcus looked like a lost puppy, or a kid who had just broken his favorite toy, and tears were welling up in his eyes. "He probably can't bear the thought of life without me," Norma thought to herself, smiling a little as she did.

"Sure," she gently said, and let her stalker in.

~~~

What was Milton going to tell her? Norma was a smart girl, and he didn't want to insult her intelligence by making up some half-baked story about how he was just wandering by, and happened to fall under her bushes. That would be ridiculous.

So it was the moment of truth.

Norma opened the door to her apartment. There she was, looking happy to see him, and yet still very vulnerable. The fact that she looked happy at all startled Milton. He had expected her to be upset with him for watching her. After all, she didn't know how long he'd been there.

Yet, hidden in that smile was the vulnerability that Milton had grown to find so endearing. He loved that even though Norma exuded confidence all of the time, he could still see the average girl that lied beneath. Despite her beauty, Norma still dealt with the same self-confidence issues that many women did, and Milton liked that. He didn't want to be in love with an egotistical sexpot.

However, Milton was powerless to Norma in more ways than one. Not only was he completely taken aback by her beauty, he was also breaking the law. "Though, since she'd invited him in, it would be hard for her to make a case," he thought to himself.

It was still something that made Milton uneasy. *He* knew that *she* knew that she had the upper hand.

"What were you doing under my window?" Norma asked Milton, while letting him in.

"I, uh, well..." he was floundering. But he knew it was going to come out eventually. Might as well just say it. Like jumping right into a cold pool, which he always found to be more startling and breathtaking than ripping off a Band-aid.

"I was watching you," the stalker said.

Norma looked confused, and it took her a few moments to process what Milton had just told her. When she understood, she didn't seem displeased. "Watching me?" she said, still failing to hide a hint of a smile. "Why were you watching me from underneath my window?"

Milton could try and turn the tables by asking Norma why she was going to kill herself, taking the attention off of him. She could lash out, offended even more than she was now, but that smile let Milton know she wouldn't do that. Of course she would want to change the topic to herself.

"Why were you trying to kill yourself?" Milton blurted out.

Norma sat there quiet, and contemplative, and Milton thought for a moment that his plan had worked! But he was wrong.

As she sat there lightly running her fingers over her wrists, the blade no longer in her hand, Norma looked like she would tell Milton everything that was on her mind, absolving him from guilt, and avoiding this impending awkward conversation. But she abruptly turned to him and said, "This isn't about me right now Marcus, this is about *you*, and what *you* were doing watching *me* through *my* window!"

"This is it," Milton thought, "You're about to lose the woman of your dreams and probably get arrested, or at least get a restraining order." Oddly though, Norma still didn't seem genuinely mad. It was almost like she was trying very hard to be upset over this whole situation.

After a few seconds of trying to read Norma's emotions, Milton decided it was now or never. If he wanted to spend the rest of his life with this woman, then it was about time that he started being honest with her. Sure, he could keep some things a secret, but she needed to know about why he was following her.

Deep down inside, Milton was petrified that Norma would do the same thing to him that his mother had: abandon him. One of his psychiatrists in the mental facility told him that he had serious abandonment issues, and dealt with it by staying distant from people. Though, through following people, he never felt alone.

Norma had broken down that barrier for Milton. She was the first person who ever truly loved him. She didn't know everything about him, but do people ever really know their partners? Everyone has little secrets to hide. His secret was just too big, and he needed to tell someone, and Norma was going to be that person. The risk of losing her didn't outweigh the amount of freedom Milton felt he could enjoy as a result of their arrangement.

"Well, I guess I should start at the beginning. It will be less confusing," Milton started.

Norma looked at Milton, with her eyes pressing him to go on. He drew in a deep breath and began.

"For starters, my name isn't Marcus, it's Milton."

A surprised look passed across Norma's face, but her gaze urged him to go on with what he wanted to say.

"This is a bit hard to explain, and I don't expect you to understand, and before you say anything, yes, I've been to therapy. More therapy than I care to think about. I just am the way I am, and for some reason I can't change."

Norma stared at Milton after this odd proclamation, still wanting him to go on, but looking more confused. He knew he had to continue, and fast.

"You see, I have this compulsion." Milton paused. He knew how this would sound, but he had to make her understand that it was perfectly fine. "It's an odd one, I know, but I have this compulsion to, uh, well, I like to watch people."

Norma just kept giving Milton the same eager stare, urging him to go on. It was nearly unwavering, save for the occasional flickers of shock in her expressions.

There was something about that look though, and Milton considered whether or not he should tell her anything else. Then it was like the floodgates opened, and Milton spilled out years worth of stories and realizations that he'd kept to himself all of this time.

Things no one else had known, like the first time he'd followed his mother around. Milton told Norma how it was unlike any TV program he'd seen or any book he'd read. He was seeing her mother at her most vulnerable, when she thought it was just herself in the mirror, and no one else.

Milton had observed that his mother felt more at ease, and simple. She quit putting on airs and was just his mother, dancing terribly to 80s music and not worrying about sucking her stomach in. All over the giant master bathroom (which was the size of some peoples' homes) she'd dance, while Milton watched from inside her closet, behind the dirty clothes hamper.

Later on in life, Milton would have the tough awakening when he realized that not everyone's dirty laundry smelled as good as his mother's; it was like she wasn't even capable of sweating.

Everything smelled just like her perfume, which she had flown in specially from Italy.

Milton told Norma about the first time he'd followed a man, and how traumatic it was. Here he was, expecting the quintessential family man, and he got a homosexual philanderer. He reiterated to Norma that it was the cheating that bothered him, not the fact that Johnny preferred men.

At some point, after he talked about Jenny, Milton completely forgot Norma was there. It was like every thought and feeling he'd pushed aside, for the sake of being objective, had been brought forth. As though he remembered every biased thought he'd ever had.

When he reconnected with the present, and realized that Norma was still sitting here in front of him, hearing all of this, Milton looked to her for some kind of reaction. There was a bit of shock in her eyes, but no horror or disgust, like Milton had expected to see.

After what felt like hours, Milton had expected Norma to be bored, but when he finished spilling his guts, exhausted and breathless, she just stared at him. He was trying to read her, but couldn't, and began wondering what *he* would think if someone had just unloaded all that on him.

After it was quiet for what seemed like forever, Norma finally piped up.

~~~

Typically, Norma couldn't stand hearing anyone talk about themselves for very long, but this time was different. This was the man she loved, or at least thought she loved, but it still felt like she was meeting him for the first time.

And besides, she found it hard to believe that anyone could be more interesting than she was, but Norma supposed that Marcus was a close second. She knew he said his real name was Milton, but she thought it was an ugly name, and Marcus fit him better. It was more mysterious, which was how she saw him.

A mystery man with a crazy past.

Norma intently listened to everything Marcus said, hanging on his every word. This was better than any movie because it was real life. She had no idea that all of this time she had been dating such an exciting man.

When Marcus got to the end of his story and told her

about when they met, Norma was flattered. She knew that something this odd, and out of the ordinary should have freaked her out, but it didn't. It only made her love him more.

All of this time Marcus had been sneaking around, watching Norma's every move because he couldn't get enough of her. Marcus was a man completely obsessed with her. Her knew all of her secrets, when she'd lied to him, what her habits were, he'd even seen her do things she'd never consciously do in front of him, like burp. Or dance around in her underwear. Or play with that one fat roll she couldn't seem to get rid of.

And he still loved her!

~~~

Milton had told Norma about everything. All of it. Every detail, no matter how embarrassing. Well, except for one thing. Now, the tricky part was how to get around the topic of the journals. He knew that he'd have to stop following her once the journal was full, but he couldn't let her know that.

Norma had to think that he'd follow her no matter what, until death parted them. He intended on being in a relationship with her, and staying loyal, but the issue of following her could not be changed. There was no way around it. But only being with her during her normal hours would have been unacceptable now. Now that Norma knew about him and his compulsion, she'd require all of his day to be surrounded around her.

In the awkward silence, noting that he'd been noticeably thinking very hard, Milton blurted out, "To hell with this journal. I love you Norma. I love you so much. You're the woman I want to follow to the ends of the Earth. Journal or no journal. Only, I need you to stay with me. I can't live without you."

That last bit was the truth because he did want to be with her, but more importantly, not finishing a journal would drive him mad.

~~~

Norma had every intention of staying with Marcus, especially after his proclamation of love, but she couldn't let him think that. She had to play with him a bit.

This would be her greatest performance ever!

"Marcus," she started, acting indignant. "I don't even know where to begin. You expect me to believe this?

You want me to believe that you've been following people for years, living off your *fortune*?"

Norma always made sure to make mention of Marcus' fortune, because it was something that was always in the back of her mind. It wasn't that she only dated men for their money, but she liked to live comfortably, and she didn't like to work.

In order to reel Marcus in for good, after that confession, Norma would have to play some hard-to-get. She eventually continued, "We both know what you are. You are just a creepy, *creepy* man who conned me into loving him for his own benefit. You wanted to stalk me, and thought using me *sexually* in the meantime seemed like a good idea"

Norma felt that now was the perfect time to turn on the waterworks, gradually, of course, ending with huge, body-shaking sobs.

"All this time, I thought you loved me, but you were really just leading me on. What was I to you? Just some science experiment?!"

Marcus started to answer Norma, but she cut him off. He'd had his turn to talk; this was her monologue.

"No. You don't get to talk. In fact, you don't get to do

anything! You don't get to see me again, you don't get to talk to me, or take me to dinner, or hold my hand, or come to this apartment. Ever. Again."

She started sobbing big, heavy sobs, complete with dramatic gasps of air.

"As a matter of fact, *Marcus*, or whatever your name is, you need to get out. Now! That's it. Stand up. Get out! I don't want you here anymore. Ever. I never want to see you again. And if I see you around here, I'll call the police."

Marcus was shocked, hurt and stuttered as he slowly, but obediently stood to leave. He tried to say words, but nothing was coming out except for sounds. Clearly, this had exactly the affect on him that she wanted.

Through her tears, Norma said, as she pushed Marcus out the door, still caught up in the emotion of it all, but remembering the lines she'd made up for herself, "I really thought you could have been my one true love."

Norma slammed the door, and with her back to it, and slumped to the floor in a pile. She cried even harder and louder than before, shaking her body to the core, and yet through the tears she was smiling.

~~~

Milton was devastated. He wanted to cry so badly, but no tears formed. He felt like his heart was being ripped out of his chest, and knew this must be what heartbreak feels like. He'd always heard about it, seen it in some of his subjects, but he figured they were being dramatic.

Now that he'd experienced it for himself, Milton knew there was nothing dramatic about being physically ill because of your feelings for someone else. He felt like he was falling, sinking into a hole. In fact, he stopped and looked around. Milton had no idea where he was.

Milton's feet had been moving but his brain was consumed with Norma, and he'd been carried away to a place he was unfamiliar with, both mentally and geographically. Finally admitting that he was lost, the heartbroken lover knew he should find the way back to his car, but he couldn't bring himself to care about that.

So he did what any reasonable person would do, and found a bar. Milton didn't know what part of town he'd wandered to, but he knew that if there was alcohol, it was the next best thing to finding his car. Probably better since he shouldn't be driving in this condition if he couldn't even walk.

The place that he found was a dive pub, The Horse and Hound, which was directly across the street from him, its lights like a beacon for the lost. Milton wandered over.

Typically at a bar, Milton would sit in the back, giving him the best view of everyone, so he could people watch without being bothered or noticed. But right now he wasn't thinking about others around him. All that was on his mind was Norma.

Beautiful, sweet, vivacious Norma, who he would probably never talk to again.

Sitting down at the bar, Milton finally caught his breath and began to organize his thoughts. Just when he started, the bartender came up to him.

"What'll it be buddy?"

The words startled Milton. He wasn't sure why.

"Uh, yeah, just give me, uh, whatever you have."

"We have everything. You want a beer? A whiskey?"

Milton looked up at him with what must have been the most lost look in the world, because the bartender gazed back with pity and said, "I'll fix something up for you."

Gratefully nodding at him, Milton began retracing the night in his mind, which turned into reliving his entire relationship with Norma.

From the beginning, the lover knew that he couldn't tell Norma about following her, and that he had to keep in mind what this was all about. The journal. Observing the human condition. He had to finish the journal. But he hadn't yet completed his task, and now he had no one and nothing.

Milton despairingly laid his arms on the bar and put his head in them. As his body doubled, he felt something hard in his breast pocket and remembered the journal was still *with* him at this moment.

"Screw this shit," he said out loud, ripping the book from his coat pocket and slamming it on the bar top just as the bartender brought him his drink.

It was a dark brown liquid in a lowball glass with ice, and Milton tossed it back, feeling something cold slide down the back of his throat, but not taking any time to taste it. He didn't know if this drink was strong, but he did know that just one of anything wasn't going to be enough for what ailed him.

What did people drink when they were heartbroken? When they found out the love of their life hated them in unfathomable ways? And because of all of this, you now loathe yourself too? Was there a drink for that?

The bartender turned toward Milton, evidently surprised that the drink was gone.

"Another?"

Milton nodded yes.

His thoughts were still a jumble. Norma had listened so intently to the explanation of why Milton had followed her, that Milton was sure she was okay with everything. Shocked, yes, but not furious. Not mad enough to kick him out of her life. His methods of observation had never been worse.

At some point though, Norma had loved Milton, hadn't she? And if she really loved him, wouldn't she be able to deal with what he had told her? After all, that was the real him. Or did Norma expect him to be someone he's not for the rest of his life, just to make her happy.

The longer Milton thought about that possibility, he realized that's exactly what people in many relationships want. They're a blending of two people, which inevitably means both people giving up things to make their lives fit together.

Thinking about this concept, Milton continued to knock back the liquor, and he was really starting to feel it now. He knew his assessment of relationships was correct, but it was impossible for him to give up his compulsion to follow people. He'd tried his whole life, even when he was in that mental hospital. It just never took. This was who he was and what he did.

Couldn't Norma just *try* to understand that?

The bartender returned with a drink, which Milton also threw back, and ordered another. Then he started opening up to the bartender, pouring out his soul.

"I know you see this all of the time. Well, I don't *know*, but I'm sure you do. You're a bartender after all! I'm just another guy coming in to drink away some failed relationship. But this isn't like the others, guy, let me tell you. This was love, true love, the kind of love that hurts even when you're with the person. This was the love that movies are made of, the kind that you can't just give up on," Milton soliloquized.

The bartender looked at him and said something that Milton figured he said a million times before, "Then why are you here telling me?"

No matter how cliché, that hit home, and Milton stood up, pointed at the man and said, "You are exactly correct."

He paid the bartender, tucked his journal back into his coat, saluted the wise sage, then staggered out.

Milton took one look around and realized he still had absolutely no idea where he was, and even less of an idea what he was going to do, but at least he knew where he was going.

He hailed a cab, gave the driver Norma's address and away they went.

When the driver pulled up to Norma's building, Milton popped his head up and stared outside. The four-story Mission-style apartments wavered in front of him, making it impossible to focus on just one thing. He was drunk; even he had to admit that to himself. But he was just sober enough to know not to go in there like this. Nothing good could come of that.

"You getting out or what, buddy?" the cab driver interrupted Milton's inner dialogue.

The answer to that question was easy though. There was actually no way that Milton was physically going to get out of that car.

"No. Take me to a different address. I'll give you $300," Milton said back.

"How far we goin' for 300?"

"Exactly 47.4 miles away from here. The $300 is for your time driving there and back."

"Where to, boss?"

Milton hated spending his money on things like this, but he wanted to be home. For $300 he could have easily stayed in a hotel near Norma's, and near his car, but Milton just needed to be home.

~~~

Sure, Norma was sad, but she knew they weren't really broken up. Marcus would be back for her in no time. He had to obey his obsession to follow her, didn't he? She had seen it in his eyes that he was deeply hurt by her declaration. There weren't quite tears, but it was pretty close. More important than tears was that he believed her. It had certainly been her most convincing performance yet.

Now all that Norma had to do was wait for Milton to come back, and she'd be on the lookout for him. Creeping in the bushes. Peering through her windows. Following her on the street. She'd see him.

And now when Norma was out, at Farmers Markets, or the mall, she wouldn't think she was crazy for seeing him everywhere. Because he was there. Watching her every move.

This turned her on more than she could ever have believed.

Norma also realized that now was her chance to really work on her acting skills. She wanted to make Marcus think that she was totally fine without him, and that she had moved on.

Of course, she would be crying inside, wanting him to cuddle her at night and kiss her cheek to wake her up every morning. But she wouldn't let him know.

This would certainly outdo her latest, greatest performance. Maybe she would even become a method actress as a result, Norma thought to herself.

~~~

Milton missed Norma horribly. He tried to separate himself from her, and view her as a subject, like he had been able to do with all the others. But she wasn't just one of the others. She was the love of his life, and it was completely his fault that she hated him

Despite this information, Milton still had to follow her. So, every morning when he got out of bed. It wasn't him, Milton, that got him up, but rather his compulsion, his disease. If he missed a day, it really *would* be the worst thing in the world.

Sure, he had Norma's schedule memorized by now, and she was a pretty predictable creature of habit, but anything could happen in the course of a day. Someone close to her could die and he'd miss her reaction. Or what if she landed a major role she tried out for?

Milton felt a painful pang of sadness when he realized that he wouldn't be there to celebrate with Norma. He could have a small, internal party about it, but he couldn't tell her how proud he was of her, and how deserved it was, and take her out to dinner with a ridiculously expensive bottle of champagne, but not quite the most expensive in the place either.

None of that would happen anymore, and that was almost enough to push Milton right back into the bed. But he got up, got dressed, skipped breakfast because food had no taste anymore, and he headed out to go see his lovely Norma.

Milton wondered how much longer he could experience this. It was a mix between pleasure and pain, elation and frustration. But what was the worst was that the journal was almost done.

It wouldn't be long now until Milton had to leave Norma and add her story to the stack of journals sitting in the corner of his large, empty house. There was one thing he could be sure of though: that he would never fall in love with a subject again.

The pain was agonizing and fully encompassing, and it was only exacerbated when Milton realized that he'd left his car an hour away. He called a cab again. Hopping in, he explained what he'd explained to the man the previous night, and off they went to pick up his car.

Milton didn't even realize he had already driven to Norma's apartment by the time he got there. He was on autopilot. Sitting outside the building, he collected his thoughts and prepared for the day ahead of him.

As he sat out there, looking at Norma's window, Milton found himself slipping back into his memories. This hadn't happened since he'd started following Norma because he wanted to be involved in every moment and soak in all of her Norma-ness, but now, sitting outside of her home, he saw something that drew him back to his childhood. To a moment that he felt most ashamed of.

~~~

Milton realized he had a *need* to be with his mother at young age, but it was a subconscious realization. It was an obsession, really, and it led to one of the worst things he'd ever done, and he wished he could forget.

When he was very, very young, Milton would find ways to get his mother's attention, by crying or breaking things. He'd faked many illnesses to get her to drive to the school and make a special trip to pick him up. Then she'd whisk him away without stopping for any errands and tuck him into bed. She'd make him soup, put a cool cloth on his forehead and stroke his hair, singing softly until he fell asleep.

It wasn't always the same song, though Milton did realize that his mom liked a lullaby called "All The Pretty Little Horses" more than the others. It was haunting and yet, somehow so cheerful, and within minutes, Milton would be asleep. Later on, he realized why, because his mom was constantly dreaming of a different life; a better one. A life that didn't involve him.

When Milton was in first grade, his parents sat him down to tell him some "exciting" news. He was going to have a brother. His mother beamed with happiness, and his father contentedly smiled as he patted her knee, but Milton could not be more displeased. He simply got up, walked to his room, and shut the door.

For the next few days, Milton's parents tried to talk with him and tell him what a blessing a baby was, but he didn't understand and began to demand even more attention. He was only six years old, so he couldn't have known exactly what he was doing, but Milton knew that he did not want a brother, or any baby to take his mother's attention away from him.

When his mother's belly was too big to pick him up, that's when Milton really got upset and he did not want this new *brother* around. The baby wasn't even here yet and Milton's mother's time was already being taken away from him. Something had to be done.

Milton was too young to understand babies, and where babies came from, but he was old enough to feel anger, and that is a dangerous emotion at any age.

Since he was told the baby was *in* his mother, and a part of her, Milton rationalized that he was angry with his mother's entire being. He started acting out and disobeying her, hoping that the baby would feel how upset his mother was feeling and that the baby would be sad too.

Then Milton realized that if he physically hurt his mother, he would physically hurt the baby.

Mother's belly had grown too large for her to even to see her own feet, let alone the ground right underneath her. So, young Milton set up his toy cars on the stairs. He'd been told a million times not to because his mother could fall. His father had even spanked him and sent him to his room on several occasions, explaining that his mother needed to take care of herself, and falling would be dangerous to the baby.

So, Milton carefully set them up on the stairs, taking care to put his Ferrari just so, and the police car right in the middle. Each vehicle played a part in this moment. Then, he walked to the bottom of the stairs and started crying. He bawled and screamed so loudly that his mother came running out of her room and flew down the stairs.

As she did, Milton's mother stepped right on top of one of the cars. She didn't slip on it, but it hurt her badly enough so that she reflexively grabbed her foot, which caused her to lose her balance, which was already wavering from the large load she was carrying.

Milton's mother went tumbling down the stairs, eventually landing in a motionless heap at the bottom. Milton laughed, as any child would laugh at someone falling. It really was funnier than he thought it would be. But then his mother wasn't moving. He walked over to her, his little hands shaking her, and pleading with her to say something. His parents had taught him about 9-1-1, so he dialed the number and explained the best he could what had happened.

Milton walked back over to his mother, and sat down with her, holding her big hand in his two little ones. He kept kissing it saying, "You're okay mommy. You're okay." He wasn't concerned because he didn't quite understand how dangerous the situation was for his mother; he was just focused on the fact that now he didn't have to have a baby in the house.

The ambulance came, and Milton got to ride inside. They told him his mother would be fine, which made the experience that much better, because as long as she was fine, it meant his plan was working, but it also made him worried that the baby might survive.

When they arrived at the hospital, Milton had to sit outside of his mom's room, and he waited for his father, who came rushing in, asking what happened.

He told Milton to wait outside, and went into the room. Milton saw his parents hug and kiss, then his mother said something and both of them started crying.

Milton guessed they were saying that he wouldn't be having a little brother, and he smiled.

His parents stayed in there for awhile, and Milton got bored waiting. But eventually his father came out, brusquely grabbed Milton's hand and led him to the car.

When he got home, his father made Milton throw all of his toy cars away. Milton figured this was a small price to pay, even if it was an unfair one, to make sure that no one would be taking his mother's attention away from him.

As he grew up, Milton knew the incident wasn't entirely his fault, because he didn't understand that the baby was a human life, but he still felt guilty. Most of all, he felt guilty because after the baby was gone, Milton reveled in his mother's attention, which he got even more of since she was so grateful for the one son that she did have.

This is why when Milton saw Norma with another man, he had to suppress the rage and jealousy that he felt boiling up inside himself.

~~~

Milton wouldn't take a life now. He'd been to too much therapy to let his emotions get the better of him in that respect again. But when he saw Norma with this tall, handsome, well-dressed man, it took every fiber of his being not to plot the man's demise.

Jealousy was one hell of an emotion, and it had actually taken Milton years to realize what it was, and how it took over his life. As an adult, he had learned to control coveting things. He had everything he needed and what he needed was enough. Over the years that had become his mantra to battle his crippling jealousy.

This was especially important in his 'profession' (Milton knew it wasn't a profession, but sometimes he wasn't quite sure what else to call it since when observing, Milton was nothing if not professional) because he'd see a lot of things that other people had which he wanted. But when that feeling crept up,

Milton was quick to shut it down.

This time though, this time was different. Milton required even more inner strength than usual since he knew that he was going to have to follow this couple around all day, and see this handsome man flirt with his lover. The emotions welled inside of Milton, and he did everything to push them away. It was working enough to continue with the quest, which he desperately wished he could abandon at this point.

~~~

Norma knew that Marcus was somewhere. She didn't know where, but that was the point, right? She wasn't supposed to know he was even there, so she should just act like she was alone. Well, alone with Kevin.

They had met at their acting class, and Kevin had been dying to take Norma out for the longest time. Every week he asked, in different ways of course, and every week she turned him down. It didn't matter if he invited her to dinner, a movie premiere, horse riding, or even on a helicopter ride.

~~~

When Norma eventually told him she had a boyfriend, Kevin was incredibly crestfallen. He was the type of guy that had been fat, acne-ridden, and unpopular in high school, but grew up to be handsome, well-built, and affluent. So he still fawned over women, like the fat kid in him would have, but Kevin hooked them easily because of his looks.

Kevin's problem was that he was *too* nice, and *too* good looking. Women couldn't believe he was the real deal. In this case, nice guys always finished last. He didn't want that to happen with Norma, but it seemed like it would. He was determined to try not to let it though.

Kevin finally had Norma out on a date for the first time, and now she was going to fall for him. He'd planned out the most perfect date. Well, the most perfect *day* date. He figured it would seem more genuine if he asked her out in the daytime and less of an attempt at being her rebound.

Kevin really did like Norma, but he'd take what he could get, even if that meant being a rebound. It wasn't his first choice, but he'd do it. So, he'd planned a romantic day, keeping the hope in the back of his mind that he would be able to drag it into the evening.

~~~

Norma didn't really care what they were going to do

as long as they had an amazing time. She planned to be fully engaged with whatever Kevin was talking about, focusing all of her attention on him, and laughing at his jokes and whatever horribly boring stories he was going to tell her. She knew this was going to be difficult because the few times she had actually talked to Kevin. he'd been about the least interesting person in the world. He grew up on a farm and liked to talk about all of *those* stories.

There were few things that Norma had less interest in than barnyard tales. Kevin had said something about a hay bale, and falling and breaking his leg, and that was why he now walked with a limp. Norma had to ask him to clarify it for her about three times because even a tale as scary as that sounded like listening to the sun shine.

Norma had no interest in any of these stories, but knew she had to fake it. For Marcus.

That would be the hardest part, Norma knew, in the back of her mind. She would have to at least believably look like she was having a great time with this turtle, so Marcus could see that she was doing just fine without him. Deep down though, Norma knew that she wouldn't be able to fully push her longing for Marcus to the back of her mind. She'd know he was there, and worse, she was going to have to listen and make conversation with Kevin, but she knew it would be worth it. Norma kept reminding herself of the intense jealousy that she would be causing Marcus. That he'd be somewhere hiding in the bushes, or maybe at the table next to them. Just like when she'd met him.

No, surely he wouldn't be that brash. She'd made it clear that she didn't want to see him again and she doubted that he would show up anywhere near her.

They met up at the bar on her corner, then walked down the street to a restaurant. Just then, Kevin grabbed Norma's hand.

~~~

Milton almost lost it. Right there. The day had barely started and he had already almost jumped at the Mr. Handsome from his hiding place. Milton knew he'd win the fight which made it even worse, and slowly he realized that he wasn't ready for this.

Milton waited until the duo had passed him, then headed back to his car. Watching Norma holding this man's hand, and enthusiastically laughing at him made Milton hurt in a physical way, as though he'd been socked in the gut. This alone was an odd sensation for him, considering that Milton thought he would probably die a single man. Now that he'd lost Norma, it still may be the case.

As important as Milton knew it was to follow Norma today, while she was on her first date after the breakup, he couldn't bring himself to do it. He couldn't get his head to wrap around the science and the mission of the journal; his heart wouldn't settle down either. If he stayed, Milton knew there was a good chance that something bad would happen. That he might lunge at the man, which would be bad because then Norma knew he was still following her.

Milton's heartbreak wasn't mended enough to continue with his cause. All he needed was some time, Milton told himself. Some time to heal enough to follow her and finish off this journal. So he went home, as Norma turned the corner. He thought she saw her look around, like she was searching for someone, but decided that it was just wishful thinking.

So he drove home, and laid in his bed for the next three days.

~~~

Norma kept casually looking around for any sign of Marcus. It was thrilling to know that she was being watched and obsessed over by someone other than her date. She knew it shouldn't be, but it was.

The more she thought about it, the more Norma realized she was living the average woman's dream. Didn't everyone want to have a man who worshiped the ground she walked on? Wasn't that what love was all about? For her, it was.

Norma started wondering why everyone doesn't want a stalker. Being the object of someone's complete attention was all that she could hope for. But no matter where she looked, she didn't see Marcus. He really was good at this.

It seemed like no time had passed at all, and they'd arrived at their destination. Kevin had taken Norma to a cute, little Italian place that she hadn't even noticed before. It was sweet, and if she hadn't been in love with Marcus, she thought a classy move like this might even draw her into Kevin a little more.

But Norma's heart and mind were still consumed with Marcus, and she looked around the restaurant for him, as nonchalantly as was possible. Apparently it wasn't as casual as she thought.

"Are you looking for someone?" Kevin abruptly asked, letting a bit of annoyance in his voice sneak through.

Norma was caught off guard. "No! No. I'm uh... Just

taking in everything here." Norma realized she'd thought about how cute the restaurant was, but she hadn't said it out loud. No wonder Kevin was feeling frustrated! "It's so beautiful! I love the decor! I was actually just speechless for a moment.." She thought she had salvaged that pretty well, as she flashed him a bright, sincere smile.

Smiling had always come easy to Norma. She didn't have to work hard at it like some of the other girls she knew. They'd always complain, wondering why men didn't like them. She'd always say it's because they forgot their smiles at home. So even when it wasn't genuine, a smile was easy to fake.

That was part of the reason Norma flourished with her girlish movie roles because that's the attitude people expected her to have. They didn't care that there was a real woman in there, who had feelings other than 'happy' and 'horny.'

~~~

Kevin didn't believe a word of what she'd said. Norma had seemed distracted nearly the entire day, and she'd laughed way too hard at the punchlines of his terrible jokes, like she wanted to make sure everyone around her knew she was having great time. In fact, some of the bad jokes Kevin had slipped in there on purpose just to see if she was even paying attention.

She laughed just as hard at those as his genuine jokes. But he still didn't care. Norma was here with him now, so he was going to enjoy himself. At the very least he could look at her beautiful, beaming face, even though it was very clearly distracted.

~~~

She wasn't sure what it was, but something inside Norma realized this situation for what it was: a farce. She was being the mean girl that she never wanted to be, and it crushed her. Sure, Kevin wasn't the man she wanted, but here he was, making her day better, and she couldn't even bring herself to listen to his stories, though, in her defense they were extremely dull.

Snapping out of her Marcus-obsessed daze, Norma looked right at Kevin, becoming completely involved in the story he was currently telling about the one time that he went outside in the snow and found a penny. The moment she started doing this, she immediately regretted it.

Kevin *was* actually as boring as Norma had feared, but she didn't want to be rude either. She knew that one day she'd be a famous actress and wanted all her former lovers to have only positive things to say about her. If she kept ignoring him, he was bound to resent it sooner or later, and that was something she couldn't handle.

Putting on a genuinely fake smile, Norma listened intently to Kevin's stories about feeding his childhood pig, and how devastated he was when they ate it one Christmas morning, in the form of both bacon and ham. Rather than feeling sorry for child-Kevin, she was completely appalled at the situation. How awful that people kill and eat their own animals! It was one thing to eat someone else's, but your own? That seemed so barbaric.

But Norma just smiled and said, "Oh, that's awful! What a mean thing to do."

She continued talking to Kevin throughout the meal, turning the conversation to something more interesting: herself. Norma told him all about how she was going to be a famous actress, and that she had no family to support her, but she'd found a way to make it in this hard world. That no matter what, she was going to shine!

~~~

Kevin found Norma to be even more self-obsessed than he originally thought. She had a glazed over look during his stories. He'd even made up some tale about having to eat the family pig for Christmas. That one at least seemed to get her attention, but barely. Her own stories consisted of Norma blabbering on about herself, in long monologues, as though she were giving a speech at her own funeral. Then again, Kevin supposed if he looked like her, he'd talk about himself that much too. Why even bother with anything else?

The longer Norma chattered on, Kevin realized all he really wanted to do was sleep with her. He thought he was above being one of 'those' guys, but realized that he wasn't. As that realization set in, Kevin became more and more comfortable with the idea of using this woman only for his gratification. After all, isn't that what was happening on this date anyway? It was clear that Norma didn't like him; he was just a captive audience for her. He promised himself that he would get as much gratification out of this date as she would.

Norma had tons of sex appeal, but not much else once you got to know her. She was like walking desire, but when she opened her mouth, all that changed. And yet he still wanted her.

Kevin now understood what all 'those guys' whom he despised meant, and he felt bad for it. He felt sad that he could be that shallow about this beautiful person, but he was. She reminded him of a saying his mother used to say to his sister:
"You're so pretty. Just stop talking."

That should have been Norma's motto. Kevin started rethinking the rest of their date. Maybe he could cut it short and just set up a date on a different day, at a time later in the night, when he'd have a better chance at getting lucky. He was ashamed at himself for thinking this way, but every time he looked at Norma, he knew that no one could fault him for it.

~~~

Norma was starting to like this Kevin guy. He was sweet, a good listener, and he was obviously interested in her. Most importantly, he was hot enough to make Marcus jealous when he took off his shirt. She was sure that Marcus would be watching her once she was inside the apartment; especially if she brought a man with her. She didn't want to have sex with him, but it was obvious how badly Kevin wanted her, so she would just make it look like things were happening between them.

There would be no way Marcus could contain his jealousy.

Norma's thoughts now drifted to Kevin's six pack, as her eyes slowly came to rest on his muscular torso, which she could see the outlines of through his shirt. They'd once done a skit in acting class where he was a handsome ranch hand. Apparently this character wasn't too much of a stretch for Kevin since he already had the body for the part. Norma noted that he had some odd stretch marks on his sides, but she could get over that once the lights were off. Then all she could do was feel his abs.

~~~

Milton sat in bed for three days. He couldn't move, "paralyzed with love," he thought to himself. "Or heartbreak." Or whatever this pain was he had, it wasn't a real pain, like one that doctors can treat; his soul hurt. Milton knew that he shouldn't have told Norma all those things about his true self, but it was too late to worry about it now. The damage had been done, and he was realizing that he may never be loved for his true self, only what he let people see.

Lying in bed, staring at the ceiling, Milton began to make shapes out of the drywall patterns, as if they were clouds floating across the sky. He found this oddly therapeutic, and at the very least, it was a way to pass the time.

Two splotches in the northwest corner turned into a small elephant, while another two blobs right above him merged to create a coffee cup.

Drawing these parallels, Milton couldn't help but to reflect on all his therapy sessions, and wondered what a Rorschach specialist would think of the creations he was making on his ceiling. It probably meant he was still disturbed. It always meant that he was still disturbed. If he said the ink blots looked like kittens and cupcakes, he was still a danger to himself.

As a child, Milton started to wonder if they just wanted to keep him in the mental hospital, until they let him out on a day which had been predestined months prior. They just told him that progress in his sessions would speed up his release date. They lied.

Now, the only difference between being home and being in the hospital was that at home he wasn't heavily medicated. He was supposed to be, but he hated the comatose feeling pills gave him; like he was walking through all of his days in a haze.

Milton had been going out and observing people for years while he was on his drugs; just sitting there, watching them with, while functioning just enough not to drool on his shirt.

Until one day, Milton stopped taking his meds. He'd decided for himself that he wasn't dangerous, at least *he* knew he wasn't – not anymore, anyway – and he didn't feel guilty about not taking his pills. In fact he felt liberated, and in a funny way it made him feel like he had more control over his life. Like, the act of taking the pills was in his hands, and by not doing it, he was taking control of his life and doing what made him the happiest.

Everyone else thought he was dangerous, but he knew that he wasn't. He'd never hurt anyone again. He'd worked really hard to get to this point in his life and didn't want to let it go to waste. As an adult, he understood that killing the pool boy and the baby were bad things, though he still wasn't sure why. He'd acted on his instincts, "which is part of what makes us human," Milton had always reasoned to himself. But he understood that what he had done was wrong, and that killing people and hurting them was wrong. Following them around was quite another matter in his mind though, and no matter how many doctors Milton talked to, he could never find a legitimate reason not to give in to his natural curiosities.

So, Milton laid in his bed for three days, trying desperately to gain control of his emotions and mend his shattered heart. He wouldn't hurt anyone, but he wasn't himself in this state, and that's what scared him.

The sooner he finished the journal, the better, but it would just have to wait for now.

~~~

Kevin couldn't help but feel like Norma was just acting the part of a Girl On First Date. He felt stupid for even thinking it, and knew that she couldn't be, because that would be crazy, but he couldn't shake the feeling.

The plan was still to have a second date – that wasn't a day-date – but that date wasn't tonight, and right now, Kevin just wanted to get away from this woman and wait for this day to end. There had been one too many overly-loud giggles and an overage of hair flips for his liking.

Kevin chalked the schoolgirl behavior up to Norma being nervous, even though he couldn't imagine Norma being the type of woman who was ever nervous around a man, but there was really no other explanation for the way she was acting. She had mentioned that she'd been with her last boyfriend for awhile, and maybe he'd liked her like this, so she was still acting this way? It was the only explanation he could come up with.

When he thought about it though, the reason behind this adolescent behavior didn't matter, Kevin was done with the day, plain and simple. Then another fact became clear to him: he still wanted to sleep with Norma, and was nervous that if she kept talking, the sex appeal would begin to wane. He had to end this date, and the faster the better. If he could just get her in bed, it would be the ultimate bragging rights, but his soldier couldn't handle much more of the giggle barrage.

As they approached her door, Norma talked too loudly about what a wonderful day they'd had, and mentioned even louder that she really liked Kevin. She even reached forward and gently, flirting, grabbed the tip of his tie. Kevin felt a rush of blood, and decided to make this a quick goodbye. He sensed that Norma was drawn to gentlemen and old fashioned ways, so he simply took her hand, maybe a bit too hastily, and kissed it. He walked away, and she said she'd call him.

Walking to his car, Kevin could feel Norma's eyes on his back. Watching him walk away. He knew that he had a body women loved to look at, but that feeling still never sat quite right with him. He was always waiting for a fat joke to be hurled his way. Finally, he made it to his car, and looked to Norma's door. She had watched him the entire time, but smiled and waved flirtily as she turned her key and went inside.

Kevin hated dating games, and as he drove away he wondered how many days Norma would wait before calling him. Three days was typical, so he braced himself for that. He never knew why people needed to play these games with themselves. If both people had fun, and liked each other, why not just call right away?

Why wait, and make the other person question themselves. If they enjoyed each other's company, just keep the fun coming and speed up the next date. So imagine his surprise when he got home to find a message from Norma on his message machine.

~~~

Norma knew she should wait awhile before calling Kevin. She usually waited four days. That was enough time to set up a weekend date, and was more than the usual three-day rule. She felt that this kept them guessing, and on their toes, and on some occasions, it caused the men to have to choose between weekend plans he'd already made, and her. She LOVED when men had to choose her over something else, because they always chose her... almost always.

Sometimes the men couldn't wait and called Norma the day after their date, begging her to go out a second time. She would tell them she was busy on every day they proposed, and would end up seeing them much, much later on, but they always made time for her. The men would be so happy to see her by then, like a puppy when its master comes home; they were like putty in her hands, buying whatever she wanted and doing whatever she wanted, no matter how silly. Norma felt like a queen and thought, "This is what it will feel like every day when I'm famous."

A few times, Norma had even suggested horribly silly ideas just to see if the men would go along with them, like having her date bungee jump solo at the fair while she safely watched on the ground, or coaxing them into fights with loud strangers at the movies. There was even one time when she ended up having to bail her date out of jail because he'd fought a maître d when they wouldn't give Norma the table with a ocean view she insisted on having.

This was all so much fun for her, but the date with Kevin was not about her. It was about Marcus. She had tried to seem like she'd had the most fun anyone could possibly have with this impossibly boring man. She'd laughed too hard at his jokes, and made a big deal out of his stories, like they were the most interesting thing she'd ever heard, even though she couldn't remember one of them.

Norma found it odd that through all of this, she still hadn't gotten a glimpse of Marcus! She figured he was being more stealthy now that she knew he was somewhere nearby, writing down all the details of what she was doing. "This must be torturing him," she thought to herself.

So, she couldn't wait her usual number of days to see Kevin again. She had to see him as soon as possible, to compound Marcus's jealousy. She wanted to make him feel miserable that he'd ever crossed her. And truth be told, she wanted to get back with him sooner than later.

Once Kevin left, Norma casually went inside, making sure to smile more than was necessary, in case Marcus could see her. She looked in the mirror to make sure she was emoting that she was smitten, and smiled when her expressions looked convincing enough.

Norma looked in the mirror and fluffed herself up. Normally she would evaluate her appearance, and now she knew she had an audience so she had to look her best at all times.

After teasing her hair a bit, and applying more lipstick for her secret audience, Norma went over to her phone and dialed Kevin's number. She figured he would love to hear a message from her when he got home.

It rang, no answer, as was to be expected. Norma left the message louder than was necessary, just to make sure Marcus could hear her if he was sitting outside the window.

"Hi Kevin, it's me," Norma started. She never identified herself by name in messages, assuming that everyone should just know who she is if she is calling them.

"I had a great time with you, and was wondering what you were doing tomorrow night. My plans just changed and I can't think of anyone I'd rather spend the time with. Call me back and tell me what time to be ready. Bye!"

Norma also never gave men the option to go out with her, by asking"Let me know if that works for you," or "How's that sound?" because she knew that any man would be nuts not to want to hang out with her. So, Norma simply always told them when they would see each other. Beyond that it was their responsibility.

Norma smiled as she gazed out her window, looking at her street knowing that somewhere out there, Marcus was watching her every move, and would be driven mad with jealousy.

It was a satisfaction and happiness she didn't know she could feel.

~~~

Kevin saw the little message light blinking on his house phone and went over to it. He had a cell phone, but still liked the romance of a house phone, so he paid the extra $19 a month just to have a landline.

Figuring it was one of his friends asking to go out that night, Kevin hit play, and was astonished that the voice on the other end was Norma's. He moved closer to the speaker, as if it would make him closer to the person whose voice was coming out of it.

As the message played on, Kevin became increasingly excited that Norma had set something up for the following day, on her own. His thoughts about the entire day began to change, and through these rosy colored glasses, Kevin decided that everything had went well, despite her being horribly boring, and acting as though she was in character, but the date had gone well on his end. This message was the confirmation of those beliefs.

Abandoning any rules he may or may not have had, Kevin called Norma back, and as he dialed the numbers, he envisioned Norma waiting by her own cell, and picking up on the first ring. They would chat all through the night about everything. He would prove himself wrong that she was boring, and they would realize they both had a lot in common, and were, in fact, meant to be together.

But, as the phone rang and rang, Kevin realized that Norma was too much of a player to be waiting on a call from him. This was some kind of game that she loved to play with men. He was just another pawn in her beautiful world. He left a message, saying, "Hi Norma, I'm so glad to hear from you so soon. Tomorrow works perfect for me. I'll pick you up at eight."

Feeling sobered, Kevin reminded himself that all he wanted was to sleep with Norma. There was no need to be idealistic about a life they could build together. They were from two different worlds, but they both coexisted in one that required using other people to prove your self-worth.

~~~

While Norma wasn't getting ready for anything, she always had Marcus in the back of her mind. Currently, she was thinking about which dress Kevin would like best on her. She picked up a little red dress that she had often worn before meeting Marcus, but he'd made it clear that he didn't like it, having once called it "unflattering." She didn't want to be unflattering on a night when she was supposed to be driving him mad with jealousy.

Marcus hadn't been the type of person who let his emotions show often, but when he did, they showed in a major way. Like the time when one waiter kept staring at Norma when they were out to eat at a fancy French place. Marcus had ignored the majority of their server's obvious gazes, even as he made his way past their table.

All the while, Norma could see Marcus's blood boiling, and she saw his face get visibly redder, and then it happened. It wasn't until Marcus saw the waiter wink that he got violent, and lost it. He grabbed the man by his necktie and used it as leverage for him to pummel the waiter's face.

Some other employees got Marcus off the waiter before he could do any more damage. He'd broken the man's nose, so there was a good amount of blood on his hands and clothes.

Norma couldn't help but remember how turned on she was by the fact that Marcus would fight for her to be only his. She tried to act sad and appalled, of course, and felt that she did a pretty good job. But inside she was smiling brilliantly.

Norma loved being Marcus's, and couldn't wait for her life to be like that again. But right now, she told herself, she was going to enjoy her night with Kevin and continue making Marcus's life hell.

It briefly entered Norma's mind that seeing her with another man could make Marcus move on from the relationship faster, since he could see that *she* apparently had. But Norma knew that no matter what, she could get any man, especially Marcus.

So, she put on Marcus' favorite dress instead of her sexy red mini. She knew Kevin would love the strapless black one, with a built-in bustier, but more importantly, she knew that it drove Marcus wild. Maybe she could ruffle his feathers and get him to expose his hiding places by showing up in this.

When she thought about it though, Norma still found it odd that she hadn't seen any sign of Marcus at all. Surely he was still following her, to finish his little notebook, but had he suddenly gotten much so better at this? She used to see faint glimpses of him everywhere she went, and for the last several days, there had been nothing.

Or maybe Marcus was just so nervous before that his subconscious wanted him to give up his hiding spot. Norma had learned all about the subconscious from her acting teacher; how sometimes we say things we don't mean because we really do want to say them, we just don't know we do. This theory sounded like the smartest to Norma, so she decided to run with it.

"Something like that," Norma said to herself in the mirror.

Whatever the reason, Marcus had rapidly become good at making himself unseen. He was so skilled now, that it was like he wasn't even there. "But of course he's following me around!" Norma mused to herself. "He has to. He *said* he has to. He's definitely still following me."

Now that she'd settled the issue with herself, Norma had to choose what color eyeshadow to wear.

~~~

Kevin was feeling confident as he walked out his front door. Like nothing in the world could stop him. He'd come prepared for everything that could possibly happen or go wrong tonight. He'd thought of every excuse Norma could have in the bedroom, and he was ready. He had condoms, both latex and non-latex, and a little blue pill in case he needed some help. He was sure he wouldn't but he didn't even want to chance it with Norma.

The only other time that Kevin had an issue getting his soldier to stand at attention was in college. He'd gotten drunk at a frat party, and still wasn't very confident in his own skin. A cute girl – not a HOT one, but cute enough to earn some respect with the guys – had agreed to go back to his room with him, and both of them knew what was on the menu. However, when the big moment came, Kevin dropped trou, and nothing happened. The girl was nice enough about it, since she hadn't seemed very eager in the first place. Kevin was mortified though. Sometimes just thinking about that moment gave him performance anxiety. So, he brought the blue pills just in case he needed medicine over matter.

Kevin also brought breath spray, recalling one day in acting class when Norma was going on and on about how much she loved breath spray and that she had no respect for people who chewed gum. "All of that smacking?! It's appalling!" she had exclaimed. Most of the time in general, Norma was just tossing notions around in the hopes that someone would find her ridiculous, or intriguing, or both, and would engage in conversation with her. She just needed attention and he was going to give her more than she'd ever wanted.

The plans for that evening were very romantic, since Kevin had spent hours preparing the outing. First, he was taking Norma to an expensive French restaurant. That way she felt fancy and Parisian, but more importantly, she could see that he had money and couldn't complain about being too full later on that night, since a $20 plate got you only two snails in a place like that.

Five minutes had passed since Kevin rang Norma's doorbell. She'd yelled out that she'd be just a minute, so there he was, standing in her hallway holding a dozen roses. He wasn't sure what kind of flowers she liked, but he knew that red roses were a safe bet.

Kevin checked his pockets again, sprayed his breath spray some more and just stood there, twiddling his thumbs, reminding himself to keep his mind on the goal. He couldn't hear any noise coming through the door. Just silence. He decided to knock again.

"Just a second! I'll be right there!" Norma hollered.

"Oh. A-a-all right," Kevin said back through the door.

He still didn't hear any movement though and imagined what she was doing.

~~~

In fact, Norma was sitting at her vanity, completely ready. She was simply staring at herself in the mirror, smiling and practicing her facial expressions. First excited, then sad, then bored, then angry. This was all part of her pre-date ritual.

Norma always made men wait. It was a personal policy of hers. Men should always wait on the woman, that way, she always makes a grand entrance.

Meanwhile outside, Kevin was starting to get impatient. Maybe Norma was just stringing him along and this was another way to make him look silly. Any of her neighbors could come out in the hall and see him standing there, waiting like a buffoon. "She could be in there right now, staring at the peep hole, laughing at me," Kevin thought to himself.

He'd knock one more time, and then he was leaving. No one kept him waiting like this. As his picked up his hand to knock, the door opened and he lightly punched her in the face as his hand moved forward to knock on the door.

"Shit," Kevin thought to himself, "All of this planning, and I'm definitely not getting laid tonight."

Of course his second thought was to help Norma, which he did. Luckily she didn't seem too hurt. Her nose wasn't bleeding but she was definitely going to milk this for everything it was worth.

~~~

Norma's face stung worse than any other time she could recall. Once she got over the initial shock of being hit in the face, she knew this was an excellent time to get some sympathy both from Kevin and from Marcus, wherever he was. She was sure Marcus was somewhere, but if he'd seen a man punch her in the face, surely he'd come running, wouldn't he? He wouldn't let someone do that to her.

But Marcus still wasn't anywhere, and it was Kevin who was taking care of her, so Norma figured that she'd take what she could get, and that was Kevin, who wasn't a bad second option.

~~~

Kevin was horrified by this whole situation. As his brain and penis fought to find good and bad in this mishap, he profusely apologized to Norma as he frantically ran to her freezer to get some ice. There was only an empty ice tray, and Kevin briefly thought to himself, "Ah, she's an empty ice tray kind of girl." His ice tray was always full, ready in case anyone got punched in the nose, or if they just wanted a cold drink.

But not Norma. Every day was a mystery in her world, and she had no time to keep her ice trays prepared. At first, he cradled her on the floor, then once they both realized the nose wasn't broken – it still wasn't even bleeding – he carried her to the couch, and gently laid her down, very concerned about all of his plans going to shit over his impatience.

~~~

Norma had never been carried by a man like that
before.

"This is just like in the movies," Norma thought to
herself, as Kevin scooped her up in his strong arms,
and set her on the couch. "The girl gets hit by the guy,
the guy carries her off to take care of her. Okay, well
maybe the hitting part isn't great but I know what I
mean."

Norma smiled through tears that she was forcing out
of her tear ducts. Truly, she felt no strong sadness, but
the added pain from her nose helped keep the
waterworks going. As the throbbing subsided, she had
to at least look like she was in pain for as long as she
could make herself cry.

~~~

Kevin's mind was suddenly all over the place, since
the thought of a lawsuit had now crept its way inside
his head. If Norma had broken her nose, then she'd
very likely demand that he pay for her nose job.

Then Kevin's attention would be torn back to the
present by Norma and all of her moaning and wailing.

He gave her an ice pack for her nose, asked if there was anything else he could do, she said no. Standing there like a lost dog, thinking about the evening that likely wouldn't happen anymore, Kevin finally said, "Should we cancel our reservations?"

~~~

Norma realized that she'd gotten about all the sympathy she was going to get from Kevin. She'd thought that he seemed the sensitive type, but that was more obviously becoming a misjudgment of character. Most guys would have seized the opportunity to get close to her, but Kevin was far too awkward for that. They type of guy that struggles to show sympathy, no matter the circumstance. She wondered how he was such a good actor, even with this handicap.

Thinking about Kevin's dinner proposal, Norma looked at him, laughed and went to her mirror. Her nose was a bit red from the ice pack, but nothing that she couldn't deal with. She put the ice pack back on for a moment, then flipped a compact out of her purse, powdered her nose and stood up to leave.

Kevin apparently wasn't expecting this response, and inadvertently showed his excitement when she reached out, and gently grabbed his arm to leave.

As badly as Norma wanted to stay home, especially with her nose feeling so sore, she knew that the show had to go on. It might have hurt Marcus to see her in pain, but seeing her with Kevin would be much, much worse.

The couple got in the car, and drove away. All the while, Norma was looking in her rear view mirror for any sign of Marcus following them, but as usual, she saw nothing.

~~~

Milton sat in bed, thinking about Norma, and cursing himself for having this compulsion, this obsession with finishing the journal. He knew it was weird. It's fucking weird to follow people around. Milton knew this! Every single doctor he'd ever been to had told him so.

But no matter how hard he tried, Milton always ended up feeling a need and an urge to follow people; to complete his journals. Over time, it had become clear to Milton why he followed them: he wanted to find people who were better than the ones he knew. Better than him, his mother and father, the pool boy, Jenny. But every single subject was just as awful as the previous one, in some way or another. People, in general, were awful.

Milton thought back to some of the other subjects he had followed before, and wondered if he'd gotten involved with them, talked to them, maybe he would have felt this ache and longing before now; maybe with each new broken heart, Milton would feel the desire less and less. The overwhelming hurt that he felt right now would have been a deterrent," in much the same way that a shock collar works with a dog," he thought to himself.

It was too late to know now, and all Milton could do was just focus on the pain, hoping it would drown out his desire to finish Norma's journal. He just wanted to go back to a time when he didn't even know that this woman existed, when his life was simple and his days predictable. Well, as predictable as a stalker's day can be.

Even though he tried not to, Milton's thoughts would wander to where he imagined Norma was, and what she was doing at this very moment. He saw her at her vanity, smiling, and practicing saying things in the mirror that she'd say later to him, or rather whatever man she was dating now. Everything she had said to him when he arrived at her door, every surprised look, or sad story from her day had been carefully rehearsed to get the biggest reaction from him.

Milton knew the lines were coming, every time, and he could almost quote them, since he'd watched

Norma say them so much to herself, but this was something he adored about her. Milton thought that her need to entertain people at all times was one of Norma's most endearing qualities, and he didn't mind that she was consciously trying to evoke emotions from him; he just played along because he knew it was what made her happiest. Whenever she saw Milton emote the reaction that she'd wanted, Norma would break character, only slightly and would give a quick little smile of satisfaction, and then would overact her character a little too much to make up for it.

But it was sweet, and as much as Norma got out of their interactions, Milton got even more, knowing that he could make this beauty feel happy. He'd never been able to make anyone feel truly happy, not even his own mother. On occasion, Milton saw glimmers of pride in his mother's eyes, but he'd never done anything that had brought her pure joy. If he couldn't make his own mother happy, how did he expect to make any other woman happy?

This was part of why Milton loved Norma so much. She gave him worth that he could not give himself. Milton knew that without him in her life, to give her the satisfaction of acting out her everyday parts effectively, that she wasn't truly happy.

Or at least this was what Milton told himself, as he lay

in his bed, staring at the ceiling, thinking of what she was doing right now.

~~~

To say that Norma was unhappy was an understatement, but as with everything, it created a role for her to play in her daily life. She acted happy when she went to the grocery store, and talked to the unhappy cashiers who spend their lives asking, "paper or plastic." Playing the part of 'Beautiful Happy Girl' gave Norma something to keep her mind on, other than how truly sad she felt.

Going to the florist was another errand that Norma tried to be happy doing, even though this one was particularly tough. Norma loved fresh flowers, and thanks to Marcus, she hadn't had to buy her own flowers in ages. Being in the shop, amongst bursts of Babies Breath and perfectly puckered tulips, Norma felt increasingly alone and sad. She hadn't realized how the little things Marcus did for her, like buying flowers, made a great impact on her. Sure, they'd always made her smile, but his constant gifts were something that she'd become accustomed to.

The other day while looking at a multi-colored bouquet of roses, Norma thought of something else eye opening and terrifying: she might have driven Marcus away for good. She dropped the yellow rose she was holding, and quickly walked out of the store.

There were plenty of beautiful women in this city, who much like her, would love Marcus' constant attention. Feeling the need for an audience was the reason people moved here, so maybe, just maybe, she had actually driven away the one man who made her happier than she ever thought possible. Had her needy ways finally ruined the best thing that ever happened to her?

As Norma rode in the car with Kevin, on the way to the restaurant, she collected her thoughts, focusing on only happy things, and tried to play the part of the 'Pleasant Date.' She wanted to trick Kevin into thinking she was into only him, and make him feel like he was the only man in the room. She already had sympathy from him, after the nose incident, so why not milk it for what it is worth?

Norma tried to start with small talk. "So how was your day?" she asked, knowing that Kevin was going to tell her *exactly* how his day was. She couldn't have cared less, but this was what she figured she had to do to seem really interested in him, and not just is his attention.

"My day was actually horrible. This guy at work, he's sort of my boss, but not really. Well, he's been trying to throw me under the bus so that he'll get this promotion instead of me," Kevin said.

Norma nodded and made her most concerned face possible. "That sounds horrible. What kinds of things has he been saying?"

"Well, for starters, he told my boss that I'm a liar..."

Already losing complete interest in his story, which was actually one of his better ones, Norma gazed blankly at Kevin. She knew this was ruining her performance, but she couldn't help herself. Kevin was very easy on the eyes, but everything that came out of his mouth just sounded like the parents on those Peanuts cartoons. "Blah, blah, blahhh blahhhhhh blah blah."

Snapping back to the present, Norma caught the end of his thought, "... You know what I mean? A total asshole."

She made a disgusted face on cue. "Yes! Oh my gosh! What a horrible sounding man."

This was going to be a long night, Norma thought to herself.

~~~

Kevin could tell Norma had completely stopped listening to everything he was saying. He'd even thrown in the part about his co-worker thinking he was liar just to see if that would grab her attention. She didn't bite.

So, when Norma's eyes glazed over, Kevin started to at least have a good time, and yammered on about cliff jumping in Mexico. No reaction. He started saying how he'd banged the secretary on his boss's desk, then his boss walked in and they had a threesome. Still nothing, but the occasional, "Mmm hmmm." Then he decided to take it one step further.

"I screwed my best friend's mom last weekend. I met her at a bar near her house, but she was horrible in the sack, so I never called her back. I mean, I can't be expected to see a woman again who I have no interest in, you know what I mean? A total asshole."

"Yes! Oh my gosh! What a horrible sounding man," she enthusiastically trilled.

Kevin knew that Norma was suddenly interested in his story right then because it meant that it was her turn to talk now, and he let her. She rambled on about some auditions she had coming up, how nervous she was, and she made some flippant, half-sincere joke about how she hoped she didn't have to show the producer her tits.

They both knew she would have to. It was practically like a handshake in the industry. She could have been trying out for the part of an old, miserly woman who was sexually ambiguous, and she would have to show off the girls to get the part.

Kevin often had to do the same thing with his abs, and would somehow convince himself that it was similar to what she would go through. The sensitive fat kid inside of him told himself otherwise, but the muscular, much sexier Kevin told him to shut the fuck up and keep his big boy pants on... Until Norma took them off later anyways. He made her feel better about her flashing the director by laughing and saying things like, "Well it wouldn't be a proper audition if you didn't show him, right?"

Norma smiled, and Kevin felt that it was the first genuine smile of the evening, and suddenly he decided to change their plans for the night. The chubby, courteous kid, who truly loved women as people and not objects, had won this current internal battle, and he was going to spend the rest of their dinner making Norma feel like the only woman in the world, knowing that she would *not* be doing the same for him. Always looking over her shoulder, and gazing over his, looking for someone.

Kevin wasn't really the jealous type, but he always

wondered what the guy was like, to make this knockout long for him so badly. In fact, Kevin almost hoped the guy would turn up so he could get a good look at the man who he was competing with, and clearly losing to.

They arrived at a much nicer restaurant than Kevin had originally planned; the kind where you need reservations, which he did not have. What he did have was better: money. He didn't like to spend it, or even let people know he was a very smart investor, but there was just something about Norma, that when he let it, turned him to mush.

Kevin opened Norma's car door for her – she didn't even make an attempt to get out until he arrived at her door – and held out his arm, which she took with her delicate hands. They walked inside as the valet drove away, and Kevin slipped the maître d a $100 bill; they were seated them promptly in a secluded corner.

Norma had worked her way under Kevin's skin and in this moment, there was nothing he wanted more than to see that genuine smile she'd flashed earlier. So, he put up with her aimless rambling, smiling and nodding the whole time. There wasn't a question about if he'd get laid tonight, because she was clearly having a lovely time, but he just wondered if she *really* was, or if she was just acting again.

~~~

Finally, Milton dragged himself out of bed. He looked loathingly at the journal beside him, knowing what joys it was full of and despising it. After having a stare-off for about five minutes, which he knew he would lose from the beginning, Milton reached over and grabbed it. He hastily flipped to the end, making sure to not read anything in between.

Counting the pages and lines left, Milton guessed that if he spent one more day following Norma around, he could write enough largely printed notes to finish off the journal and have her out of his life forever.

Now there was just the matter of really getting himself out of bed and into town. Milton got up, and stretched his arms very high overhead, pulling his hands straight up, as though he were going to pull them out of his sockets. No injury was incurred, and he slowly walked to the shower. A day ago, he realized that he'd been in bed so long he was starting to give off an odor, but there was nothing he could do about it then, figuring that he deserved to wallow around in the stench of his misery for allowing himself to get involved with a subject.

The hot water felt good on his back, but Milton felt it

wasn't hot enough. The cold water knob remained unturned, but nothing was scalding enough to make him feel like he'd really gotten clean. It wasn't a dirty feeling that Milton was experiencing, but more of a longing for escape. He didn't want to be himself anymore.

Hoping the steaming hot water would melt his skin off, Milton scrubbed and scrubbed himself, wishing that after it all he would be a new person. Desperately wanting to be normal, so that he could have a normal life with a normal family and a normal job. He had cash to live off of, but he wanted so desperately to be just like everyone else, in at least one part of his life.

After showering for what seemed like an hour, Milton stepped out, feeling exactly the same as he had when he'd gotten in.

Sighing in defeat, Milton lumbered over to his dresser, pulling out something to wear. He didn't know what it looked like, and he didn't care, he just knew that going naked was out of the question. His shirt was on backwards, and his sweatpants were inside out, but "at least they are on," he told himself as he opted for a pair of slip-on shoes because he absolutely couldn't be troubled to tie a shoe right now. Any extra effort was completely out of the question.

This was careless, he told himself as he caught a

glimpse of his ensemble in the mirror. He'd chosen a red shirt with army green sweats, which was not exactly the most inconspicuous thing he owned.

"What if Norma saw the stand-out red shirt and called the police," Milton thought to himself. Then finished the thought by admitting to himself that he probably belonged in jail for all of his following anyway. That way people could save him from himself. He couldn't walk around stalking people and making journals if he was stuck in a cell for 23 hours a day. How long could a person go to jail for stalking anyway? Could he be in there for the rest of his life?

The shirt was worth the risk, because the effort to change was too great. Either way, he'd be rid of Norma by the end of the day, an he could try and move on with his life; whatever kind of a sordid life it was.

So, Milton grabbed the journal, a couple of pens in case one ran out of ink, his wallet, his keys, and walked out the front door, hoping that his life would feel vastly different by the time that he returned that night, but knowing that it wouldn't and everything would start all over again tomorrow.

~~~

"Maybe I was wrong about Kevin," Norma thought to herself as she lay next to him, looking at his perfectly chiseled body in the soft morning light. He was still naked from the night before, well, really only from a few hours before.

Norma had never been with a man who actually couldn't get enough of her. The two had gone at it like animals all night long, finishing and starting right back up again.

Norma was careful to get out of bed slowly, and she walked over to her vanity to brush out her hair and fix her makeup. It was a firm belief of hers that she needed to look perfect upon falling asleep and on rising. No one wanted to wake up with a bear next to them, and what if a man woke up in the night to steal a glance at her. She didn't want to look like a hot mess.

As Norma slowly stroked the soft-bristled brush through her hair, she furiously fought back thoughts of Marcus. It was a losing battle, she knew, because no matter what, even when she was having a better time with Kevin than she thought possible, her mind was still on Marcus.

It was actually starting to *worry* Norma that Marcus hadn't popped up somewhere by now, and she started to really second guess if she had done the right thing by 'driving him away.' She was so sure that he was head-over-heels in love with her and would have continued to follow his obsession with her, no matter what she said. "Maybe I was wrong though," she thought to herself, and started to come to terms with the fact that she was going to have to move on from Marcus, even though it seemed impossible.

Turning her head, Norma gazed at Kevin sleeping in her bed. He had the body of Adonis, and he could definitely keep her satisfied. Norma found herself beginning to wonder about his money situation, which was a sign that she was thinking seriously about someone.

With Marcus, money had been a big draw at first, but then Norma began to actually fall in love with the man, and the money didn't matter so much anymore. Obviously it still mattered a little though, because money is money, and it runs the world. She didn't love Kevin, yet, but felt that if he was flush, it might speed up the process a bit.

She thought back to the night before, when Kevin had paid the maître d to seat them right away at the restaurant, and insisted on having the chef make them a special meal that wasn't on the menu. Then he instructed the waiter to bring them a bottle of the oldest wine they had. They brought out a red wine from the mid 1900s and apologized for not having anything older. Kevin had scrutinized the bottle and year, finally making a disapproving sigh and saying it would have to do.

Norma had been surprised watching it all unfold before her. She'd had men wine and dine her before, but it was nothing like this. Not even Marcus had done anything like this, and he'd admittedly had his inheritance. Even in that moment though, when she was the object of Kevin's attention, she couldn't push Marcus from her mind.

"That's completely normal," Norma assured herself. She'd been in a very serious relationship that had run its course, and now it was time to cleanse herself of it, but it would take time. Like clothes that have gotten a bit of punch spilled on them. It took a few washes but eventually, the stain came out, leaving no remnant of the good time that was had. She'd just have to wait for that in her own life.

Norma walked towards the bed, and sat down at the foot of it, gazing at Kevin, and sorting through a million thoughts flooding her mind. Yes, she was sure that she could at least possibly love him; in time. She was also sure that he adored her because even if men's mouths could lie, their penises could not.

If Marcus no longer loved her, Norma figured Kevin was a much handsomer, and potentially wealthier version that she could give a chance.

Just then, something outside of the window next to her bed caught her eye. There was a flash of red, that she'd just been able to see in the corner of her peripherals.

"It's Marcus!" she excitedly thought to herself, half questioning if she'd yelled it out loud because just then, Kevin stirred. Norma scurried to the window, looking out for any sign of the red she just seen whiz by, but there was nothing. No sign of anyone, and as she was consumed with scrutinizing every little bit of the setting below her windowsill, Kevin came up behind her and started kissing her neck.

Norma was a bundle of emotions. She wanted Kevin to go away so she could stay right there and have a standoff with Marcus. Then part of her reminded her that it would look insane, which could chase Kevin off. There was another small part of her that just wanted to slump in the corner and be left alone. She didn't want to be with anyone right now.

The real end of her relationship was beginning to hit Norma, and it was more than she thought that she could bear. She was faced with the realization that Marcus was gone, really gone, and it was her fault. Sure, Kevin was very excited about being with Norma, but it wouldn't be the overwhelming consumption with her that Marcus had. She'd never be the full object of another man's attention like she had been before. There may be someone out there, maybe even Kevin, who would make her the object of his affection, but not his full attention. Not like Marcus.

Even in the middle of their gorgeous, decadent dinner, Norma had seen a faraway look in Kevin's eye that let her know he wasn't actually listening in that moment. He was hearing, but he wasn't hanging on her every word like Marcus used to.

There used to be a constant genuine interest in every single thing she had to say, no matter how trivial and whiny it may have seemed. Sure, it was because he was studying her, but when it came down to it, Norma didn't care. This was something that she adored about Marcus, and wondered if Kevin would ever grow to be that way as well. In her experience, people tended to get less interested in their lovers as they were together for a longer period of time, not the other way around.

Still, as she stood there with Kevin, Norma realized how crazy she must seem, always looking for a man who she was becoming fairly certain wasn't there anymore. She took a deep breath, thinking about all of the questions that were floating through her mind. Then she exhaled, telling herself that she was letting go of Marcus, and everything that he meant to her.

She was letting go of the hope that she'd still have a life with this man who gave her the attention that she so desperately craved.

But Norma was letting it all go, and with her next big breath, she told herself that she was inhaling this new life with Kevin, or at least just a new life, which she was starting to hope Kevin would be a part of. Even as she came to terms with this, she still thought that she saw another glint of red in the window, but she made herself push it far from her mind, knowing that it was time to move on.

~~~

Kevin was sure that he'd finally won Norma over. As the night went on, he'd become more and more interested in Norma as an entire person and less in just her body, although that was still a pretty big draw. He'd realized that she wasn't as distant as before, although he did catch her eyes wandering from time to time, and he wondered if it was something he was talking about, because he'd already scanned the area and knew he was the best looking man in the room.

So, clearly, Norma was just daydreaming.

When she talked, he began to find her stories

interesting as well. He wasn't sure if it was just because he was getting used to her surface conversations or if it was because he actually enjoyed talking to her. Since she had the intelligence of a high school Freshman, he was pretty sure he was just getting used to it.

After dinner, Kevin had taken Norma back to her apartment, where they went inside and he finally got what he'd wanted all along. First, he walked her to the door, like a proper gentleman. She was a bit tipsy, but not drunk, and she asked him in. Kevin found himself glad that she hadn't been wasted. A very small part of him always felt bad when he slept with drunk girls, who he was pretty sure wouldn't have slept with him otherwise.

But Norma had only had a bit too much to drink, so he let her take the lead, since he knew where it was going anyway. They had begun kissing the moment she locked her apartment door, which led to her gently pushing him onto the bed. He didn't need any cues to take off his clothes, and she'd seen him in only his boxers during acting class anyway.

Norma followed Kevin's lead now, and before he knew it, his dream for months was finally coming true. However, as with most dreams, it hadn't been quite as good as he'd expected. Like when he got a kite as a kid, and realized that without strong breeze, it wasn't much fun.

When he woke up in the morning, Kevin had every intention of seeing Norma a few more times, and then breaking it off. She was interesting enough, and certainly beautiful, but she wasn't material for the long run. "There's nothing wrong with having a little fun, though," he told himself.

As Norma sat at the edge of the bed, gazing out the window, Kevin had stirred and happily asked her how she slept. She seemed oddly distracted though – the worst he'd ever seen her – which is when an awful thought hit him: maybe *he* wasn't as good in bed as he thought he was, and she was unhappy that they'd slept together. She'd seemed responsive enough, but everything was always different in the light of day.

Kevin asked Norma if she was okay, and slowly she began to snap out of it, eventually focusing all of her attention on him. He asked if she wanted breakfast, and got up to move toward the kitchen. She went with him, tiptoeing ahead and snatching up the half-full garbage bag.

"I'm going to take this out," she suddenly and hastily told him.

"Oh-kay," Kevin tentatively told her, wondering what

was inside it. A positive pregnancy test was his first thought. Was she tricking him into paying child support? They had used a condom last night, right? No, she couldn't be. Tests didn't work like that, right? It was an issue he'd never had to deal with before.

No, it was probably just some other weird feminine product; no need to dwell on it. It wasn't like he was going to marry Norma.

~~~

Norma rushed into the kitchen, hurriedly grabbing the hardly-filled trash bag. "Kevin must think I'm a nut," she thought to herself. But she had to go outside and snoop around a little for Marcus. She knew she had seen him, and that he was still somewhere. She went to the trash cans out in the back and began to creep around the building. She quietly put the trash in the dumpster, lowering the lid as soundlessly as possible, and began tiptoeing her way around the building.

As she neared her window, Norma squatted very low. She was certain Marcus was out there, but just in case he wasn't, she didn't want Kevin seeing her and thinking she was spying on him.

Just when she began to approach her window, she peered out into the street and swore she saw a man in a red shirt walking by who looked just like Marcus. Throwing caution to the wind, Norma popped up and dashed out to the sidewalk, looking up and down the street to see which way the mystery man had gone.

When she didn't see anyone, she walked quietly back to her building's stoop and sat down to cry. She let out a few large sobs, then pulled herself together, knowing that this emotion needed to be harnessed for her next 'Pretty Girl Crying' role.

Drying her eyes, Norma came back inside, and saw Kevin at the stove, flipping bacon, eggs and pancakes. He was standing there in his boxer briefs, with his abs glowing in the morning light, and Norma told herself it was time to stop obsessing over Marcus. There was a hot man, cooking her breakfast, who liked her, who was good in bed and most likely had money. Yes, she was going to get over Marcus, starting right now.

Though, she still planned to harness her earlier sadness and use it in the future. There was no sense in letting valuable emotions go to waste.

~~~

Milton made it back to his car, certain that Norma had seen him. How could she not have? How stupid it was of him to wear a red shirt, of all things! Why hadn't he listened to better sense before leaving the house! Milton knew he had slipped up, and was certain that Norma would have called the police. She'd been so furious with him the last time they spoke that there was no way she hadn't called anyone.

Right?

Debating with himself, Milton thought for a brief moment that Norma still loved him and might welcome him with open arms after his absence. Then reality set in and Milton reminded himself again that Norma thought he was a crazy man and would call 9-1-1 at the sight of him. Wouldn't she?

Milton realized he had been sitting and thinking for so long that he realized the coast was clear, and slumped into his car seat, relieved. He let the Hope creep back into his mind, after working so hard to push it away. The Hope that Norma still wanted him; that even though she was in bed with another man – who was SO much more attractive than him that Milton had no problem admitting it – that she would still want to be with him. That she would still come back to him, with her arms wide open.

This thought kept Milton in his car, daydreaming for so long that he had no idea how much time had passed. He figured it was a significant amount of time because the sun was higher lower in the sky, and most of the cars around him had changed parking spots.

So, he took a deep breath and looked down at his journal. There were still two pages that needed to be filled.

Milton rationalized with himself that he could fill things in after-the-fact, and just recall everything. This way he could easily fill up two pages, he told himself. But when it came to Norma, Milton didn't trust his memory. He was too disturbed.

There was too much. Too much he'd seen. Too much he'd heard. Too much he was thinking. Too much he convinced himself that he'd seen. In fact, now that he was sitting here, in his car, with a calm mind, Milton wondered if that was even a man in bed with Norma. Had he thought up the whole thing? Maybe she hadn't seen Milton and he just thought that she had.

After many thoughts flew through his head, Milton decided to go back into the alley and take another peek. He figured the worst that could happen would be that Norma would see him, and call the cops, which he'd already dealt with once, so the second time he'd be much better prepared.

Slowly, he crossed the street and inconspicuously slunk back to the house.

~~~

After breakfast, Norma and Kevin got ready for their day. They had tossed a few ideas back and forth about what they wanted to do later on. She had some really great ideas, Norma thought to herself, like taking pictures near town hall and then going to dinner.

But Kevin told her that he had some other things planned. She didn't mind being told what to do by a man. In fact, she liked being submissive, but she wished that he had at least given her suggestions more than just one second of consideration.

Kevin just said, "Aww, that's a cute idea, but maybe next time. I've got a better plan."

As Norma struggled with convincing herself that she was going to get over Marcus and give Kevin a real chance, she found herself failing to be persuasive. She asked the classic introspective questions that women ask at the beginning of a relationship (since it's assumed that every man will be there forever).

Could she handle being told what to do for the rest of her life? Was Kevin going to ignore her about everything she said? Would he ever respect her opinion?

Norma decided 'No' was the answer to all of these questions, which led her to the next issue of ending the relationship because she couldn't live like this. Clearly she was miserable and would keep being miser —

"Wait," Norma thought to herself. "What am I doing? I'm talking about leaving a man who I am just getting to know! Maybe he's just trying to impress me and the real Kevin will come out soon. If this is the real Kevin though, I'm sure I'll find out sooner than later. So, I won't have wasted too much time."

She obediently got dressed in something "casual, but nice" per Kevin's directions. To her this meant a shorter-than-usual sundress and some very high heels.

"This will be perfect no matter where we go," she told herself.

Kevin had left Norma's apartment for his own, so he could shower and get dressed, but he promised to be back in a couple of hours. So, she continued getting ready until every hair was in place and her makeup was perfection.

Still, she checked the window for any flash of red.

~~~

As Kevin drove back home from Norma's, he thought about what they'd do that night. She'd had some stupid idea about them taking pictures, or something, he wasn't sure because he wasn't really listening anyway.

Since Norma thought of no good ideas, Kevin had come up with some of his own, deciding that anything he could conjure was better than what she could. While he showered, he came up with more options. He knew that Norma only really cared about having money spent on her, and being ogled. So, he figured a restaurant on the boardwalk, with a seat outside so everyone could see her was the best option. They'd go somewhere first, like a rooftop bar so he could loosen her up. He also knew from experience that women felt like it was more of a complete, well-thought-out date if they went to more than one place.

"She's definitely one of those girls," he thought.

And if all went according to plan, by the end of the night, Norma would be drunk, and they'd spend another entire night in bed. He wanted to make sure she wasn't too drunk that she passed out though. Then again, who was he kidding, a girl being asleep hadn't stopped him before.

But Kevin was trying to like Norma, he told himself again. He was trying to see a future with her, because, she was great. And...

Well, the reasons didn't matter right now. He'd have plenty of time to come up with those during dinner and drinks. Drinks were always the worst part of the date because the woman is always initially sober, and you have to make her drink a lot, quickly. Women didn't always like shots though, because they felt it made them seem like party girls. Another tidbit Kevin had learned from dating.

Women seemed to be torn on the issue of beer though. Half of the girls he'd dated ordered beer, because they'd found that it made them more relatable to guys, since it was a 'guy drink,' or because they didn't want to seem *too* girly. The other half didn't order beer because it was man's drink and they wouldn't touch it on principle; or because they didn't want to seem too tomgirlish. Every drink had a connotation with it.

Kevin's thoughts started to wander to girls he'd been with before, and as they ran through his mind, like a film reel, he realized that Norma actually paled in comparison to them. She was actually rather plain, and fairly average in bed. Besides having an amazing body, and a seductive personality, she was pretty dull.

"So why do I care so much about being with her then," Kevin asked himself, and no good answer came to mind, but he kept on planning the date anyway.

~~~

After thinking about it long and hard, Norma decided that she couldn't go on the date with Kevin. She'd been torn about it, but figured several things. The first was that they had just started dating, so there was no need to go out two consecutive days in a row. That was moving a bit too fast for her.

The next thing she realized was that she truly and genuinely didn't feel like going out. After she slept with a man and he'd stay the night, she always felt a little dirtier. Like she and her apartment were ashamed for what had happened. This was a feeling she'd always gotten, even though it was silly. Kevin was a guy that she was dating and had known for a very long time. There was nothing to be ashamed of. But she was.

So, after a man had stayed the night, she felt a compulsive need to clean her apartment and scrub it. Go to the laundromat and wash her sheets in hot water, even if it made them fade a bit.

The last reason Norma couldn't go out was because her desire for Marcus was still too overwhelming. Despite trying to get the guy out of her head all day, she just couldn't. Every time she had finally turned her thoughts elsewhere, something would pop up that made her think of him.

Sitting on the couch, Norma started flipping channels, and then landed on some crime show about stalkers. Ironically, this had been one of Marcus's favorite shows. Knowing what she now knew, she was disgusted for a moment, thinking about how many of these episodes she had watched with him. Then the disgust quickly turned to a small feeling of flattery welling up again inside her.

Every time she thought about the fact that Marcus was utterly obsessed with her, Norma smiled. That's all she'd ever wanted was someone's complete attention and affection. Then she thought back to earlier that morning. Had she really seen him? Had he really been there? Surely a man's object of obsession couldn't change so quickly.

She became self righteously indignant for a moment and stood up, just in case Marcus was somehow watching her, as if he could read her mind too.

If Marcus was able to get over her so soon, then he didn't deserve her.

Norma made sure to say this revelation out loud, just like people in the movies talked to themselves, because she was becoming certain he was lurking around somewhere. But, she still decided not to go out with Kevin.

Picking up the phone, Norma leaned on her counter, facing her window. She nonchalantly filed her nails as the phone rang. Kevin's voice mail came on and she waited for the beep.

"Hi Kevin, it's me. I'm feeling under the weather and am going to cancel for this evening. I'm sure you understand. I'll call you tomorrow and set something up."

~~~

Kevin knew he had the upper hand with Norma, and he was going to start playing the game, so when he saw her call on his cell, he clicked ignore, and waited for the voice mail icon to pop up.

It surprised him how anxious he was to hear what she had to say. But it was a different kind of anxiousness. It was excitement, which he hadn't anticipated feeling, after realizing how utterly average this woman was.

Kevin couldn't believe it. He was actually feeling excited to see what Norma's message would be. That minute between hitting 'Ignore' and the voice mail icon popping up felt like torture, and then it dawned on him: what if she didn't leave a message? What if she thought he was an ass for not answering her call?

Panicking, Kevin wondered why he'd given in and played this stupid game. They were adults, after all. If only this was an old fashioned answering machine, he thought to himself, and he could have heard what Norma was saying, and picked up mid-message, explaining that he'd just gotten home from setting up their amazing evening together.

Just when Kevin was really starting to get nauseatingly anxious, the voice mail icon appeared. He clicked play and listened to the entire message, his countenance falling with each passing second.

Knowing that he'd messed this up, Kevin was determined to make it up to Norma. If she wasn't feeling well, he was just going to have to go over there and surprise her with some soup. She would love that kind of thoughtful thing.

~~~

Milton had found a nice spot outside of Norma's window which had such thick shrubbery there was no way he'd be seen. It was also fortunate that she had left her window open because it was much easier to hear what was going on inside. He also figured that if she'd left it open, it would mean she hadn't seen him earlier, because if she had, she'd have been totally freaked out and barricaded herself inside.

But no. There Norma was, dancing around with her vacuum, wearing nothing but her silk kimono, which was only loosely tied at the front. When she leaned over to vacuum with the hose, the robe opened in a way that he could see her breasts.

Milton had been so obsessed with finishing the journal and erasing Norma from his life that it had been easy to push the sexual things he'd miss out of his head. But now, he was sitting here, and had decided to finish the journal, which was the biggest of his decisions.

As Norma continued to unknowingly tease him, Milton's blood pumped harder, as he struggled to make himself remain calm.

"Thank God for this shrub," Milton thought to himself.

He kept right on observing, exposed to the elements. Then things got impossible.

Norma vacuumed her entire apartment five times, so after 30 minutes had gone by, Milton couldn't ignore what he was feeling anymore. He laid his journal and pen down, annoyed, and sunk further into the bushes, turning his back to the window, and grabbing ahold of himself.

He started moving his hand up and down fast, knowing it wouldn't take him long since he'd been turned on for such a great amount of time. Sure enough, about a minute later, Milton closed his eyes and exhaled.

Turning himself back toward the house, he peeked his head above the bushes, but fell back immediately with a yelp.

There in front of him was Norma, standing in the landscaped alley, staring at him and smiling.

~~~

Norma *knew* she'd seen Marcus that morning. She couldn't push it out of her head, so she continued on just like any other day when she would have seen him. Vacuuming the same spots over and over without any sign of movement, Norma was beginning to wonder if Marcus actually *was* there again, or if her mind was just playing awful games with her. She thought that Marcus should have made a little but of noise by now, and she'd have caught another peek at him. But so far there had been nothing. Looking over at the window was risky though, so Norma continued to try and look from the corner of her eye. If Marcus caught her eye again, he might leave for good and not return.

Just then, Norma finally saw some movement right under her window.

The bushes were too thick to see through, but they were definitely moving. The rustling was rhythmic, and Norma wanted find out exactly what was going on. She tied her robe on tighter and ran out of her apartment, not bothering to close any doors because that could alert him. She'd just made it to the bush as Marcus pushed his head up.

Marcus looked so shocked, she thought he might have had a heart attack, so she quickly said in a voice that was probably too loud, "It's okay! Don't worry! I'm not mad."

The next look Marcus gave Norma was even more confusing than the first. Finally, he managed to say,

"You – you mean – you're not –"

Full sentences were not his strong suit right now, so Norma stepped in and said, "No. You're fine." She paused for a moment, soaking in the way he looked, like a puppy who just got found by his master. It hadn't hit her until this moment just how much she really had missed him. Neither of them could say anymore words, so she just took his hand, helped him out of the bush and walked him inside.

~~~

"She's calling the police," Milton thought to himself. "She's calling the police and I'll be arrested and go to jail for life. Okay, maybe not for life, but for a very long significant amount of time. Definitely long enough for Norma to get married and have a family. Maybe even have grandkids by the time I get out of prison."

Milton knew that rationally, he was being irrational, but he just couldn't get the vision out of his head of him sitting in a cell. If he were locked up, by the time he got out, he'd surely be driven mad by the fact that he had an unfinished journal, just sitting there, waiting to be completed.

But Norma was smiling. "She wouldn't be smiling if

she didn't really want me there, right?!" he continued talking to himself. Though, he made a mental note of how beautiful Norma looked, standing there with the sun behind her back, lighting up her hair like an angel.

Milton was so powerless to her, that he just followed Norma inside her apartment, wordlessly (partially out of fear, and partially out of anxiety). Once he got inside, all the memories of them came flooding back to him and he cursed his compulsion that brought him back here. He saw her bed, the kitchen, the couch, and thought of all the things they'd done in this place. All of the sweet moments they'd shared.

Milton remembered the time that they watched The Exorcist together. Norma had never seen it, and afterward she was so scared that she couldn't sleep. He stayed up all night with her and talked so that she didn't feel afraid. As soon as the sun came up, they both finally rested.

Looking to the front door, Milton recalled the time he was giddy about being in love with Norma, and he kept ding-dong-ditching her apartment, while taking notes of course. On the third ring, she dramatically threw open the door and started to yell, when he hopped into the doorway with a giant bouquet of flowers.

Milton wanted to love her like that again. Freely and

to the point of silliness. He wanted the ability to be so wholly himself with another human. Without Norma, nothing felt quite the same. It was like he saw in black and white.

As Norma led him inside, she motioned to the couch, and Milton sat down. They stared at each other for a few moments. She was smiling, but he couldn't tell what kind of smile it was. "She really is a great actress," Milton thought to himself.

Milton had no idea what kind of expression he was making, but he had to imagine that is was quite amusing since she just kept on staring. Finally he broke down. "Norma, I had to come back. I had to see you again. I – I – Everything felt wrong without you."

There was a glimmer in her eye and Milton knew he was on the right track.

"I realized that I can't live without you," when he said this, he realized how cheesy it was, but it was also true, and she was eating it up.

"Not to say that I would kill myself if we weren't together," she frowned slightly as he said this. "I mean – What I'm trying to say is – I need you. I need to be with you. I need to be around you and have you in my life. Nothing feels right without you. I can't eat, or sleep, or enjoy anything. I want to share it with you."

There. He said most of what was true and exactly what he was feeling. Now Milton waited for a response from her. It seemed like he was waiting for an eternity, but it was probably only more like 30 seconds; it was the longest 30 seconds of his life.

Norma finally piped up, saying, "I've missed you too, Marcus."

~~~

Norma was touched by what Marcus had said, and she'd felt exactly the same way. During the time that he'd been absent from her everyday life, she felt like she was missing her other half.

The other thing Norma felt was a significant pride in the fact that she'd known Marcus couldn't resist coming back to her, and recognized that this was yet another chance to get a little acting practice in. Not that she was going to say things she didn't mean, but she must act how a lady should in this situation and not let her feelings get the best of her, even though she wanted to throw herself at him.

Norma said, "I've missed you too, Marcus. When you

left, I felt like a part of me was missing as well. But that made me wonder if I needed to spend some time alone. Finding myself outside of you. Unfortunately I started dating a friend – who treated me wonderfully! – but it all made me realize that if this great guy couldn't make me happy, I was doomed because I'd given my heart to you."

She knew she sounded like a script, but these words came flowing from Norma because she was letting herself be honest for once. Honesty was always the best policy, or so she was told. She continued, "At first, I was totally freaked out by the thought of you following me around all of the time. I felt like my privacy was violated and I was shocked that you kept that secret from me for so long. I was hurt, really. But I understand why you did it, because, and I don't mean to be offensive, it's completely abnormal to stalk someone."

There was a look of acceptance on Marcus's face, but more importantly he was rapt, so Norma continued, "The more I thought about it though, the more I realized that I couldn't fault you for loving me and wanting to be around me all of the time. It was a compliment more than anything that you were so obsessed with me. And I realized once you were gone, that I missed that attention. I missed being the reason you woke up and got out of the house in the morning. I was completely flattered.

"What other man would care so much about a woman, love her so fully that he would devote his whole life to studying her and learning everything about her. I realized I *want* that kind of obsessive love in my life. To never truly be alone, even when I am."

"Now is the moment," Norma thought to herself. "The pinnacle of the performance. Pausing dramatically, she added, "I'm yours, now and forever."

Neither person could hold themselves back any longer and they both fell into a full embrace. Norma had missed Marcus's hands on her body. He somehow knew right where to put them to drive her wild. This both creeped Norma out and flattered her, as did most of the things she found out that Marcus did.

Marcus' hands familiarly found their way around Norma's body, and she led him to the bed. They made love then lied there together, cuddling and staring at each other in a sweet, non-voyeuristic way, for one of the the first times that day. Norma finally felt safe again. Really, truly safe. She had the unyielding attention of a man, and she would have it for the rest of her life. Even if she got fat and wrinkly, which would never happen. "But if it did," she thought to herself, "Marcus would stay by my side and love me."

Norma fell asleep smiling for the first time in as long as she could remember.

Then there was a hard knock at her door.

~~~

Kevin stood outside of Norma's door, flowers in one hand and a plastic bag full of takeout grilled cheese and piping hot chicken noodle soup in the other. If she couldn't come to him, then he'd nurse her back to health.

The whole time he was buying the bouquet and waiting for his to-go-order, Kevin kept thinking that he couldn't believe he was doing this. He wasn't the guy who tried to impress women anymore. That was the old Kevin.

The new Kevin was all about making the ladies want *him*. He was good looking, charming and had money, so there was no reason for him to be standing outside of Norma's apartment, hoping that she'd be thrilled to see him; That she'd fall madly in love with him because of this kind gesture of his.

Kevin shifted the flowers into the same arm as the food, reached into his pocket, and grabbed his Bianca He skillfully popped off the cap with one hand, sprayed two sprays, then one more for good measure, popped the cap back on, put it in his pocket and knocked. Hastily shifting the flowers back into the other arm, he waited.

"Maybe Norma is sleeping," he thought to himself and if he woke her up, she'd hate him forever. Maybe he should just leave now and cut his losses. If he planned a phenomenal next date then he'd have plenty of chances to make it up to her in the future.

"No," the voice in his head said. He was going to stay here and knock. She needed to know how much he cares, and she needed to know right now.

Kevin knocked again. Louder this time. Then he listened closely to see if he could hear any movement inside. He thought he heard Norma's bed creak a bit, which was followed by a soft shuffling, growing closer, closer.

Staring at the blurry peephole from the outside looking in, he was sure that he'd seen a shadow go in front of it, as if someone were looking out. Kevin cleared his throat and said fairly loudly, "Norma, it's Kevin. I just came over to see how you were feeling. You seemed down earlier in your message."

No answer, but the shadow was still there.

Kevin sheepishly held up the flowers and to-go bag up to the peephole. "I brought soup!" he said, smiling, and knowing exactly how pathetic he looked. This was his one chance though, and he was in too far to leave now.

No answer still, but that damn shadow was still there. Maybe Kevin had imagined light in it's place before and there was actually no one at the door at all. She'd said was just feeling ill, not deathly, so she could have gone out and gotten herself some soup. But he'd come all this way and it didn't seem right for him to leave without trying a little harder. He knocked even louder and smilingly said in a singsong voice, "I'm not leaving here until you let me iiinnnnn."

Finally, through the door he heard her voice – the voice of an angel – say, "That's so sweet, but I don't want you to get sick."

Norma! So she was here after all! "I have the immune system of an ox," Kevin happily retorted.

"Well that's no good. Oxen died on the prairie all the time from sickness," she said deadpan, with no humor in her voice.

"Oh, well, you know what I mean." Kevin laughed nervously. "I haven't had a cold since I was in grade school," he said, trying not to let his enthusiasm waiver. At this point he was using every ounce of what he had learned in his acting class.

Finally Norma opened the door, but just a crack. Her hair was mussed, but she was just as beautiful as ever, and he couldn't believe that he was the lucky guy who got to date her. He also felt a little ashamed at how poorly he'd viewed her at first, but all that was in the past and she was going to be his queen now.

"Kevin," Norma started, and by her tone he knew she was going to turn him away. He couldn't let it happen. "I appreciate your concern, but I said I was going to be staying in tonight. That wasn't an invitation for you to come over. Though I do appreciate your thoughtfulness."

Norma was always so polite. Surely, he couldn't just leave. He was holding soup for God's sake! With his mind made up, Kevin pushed his way inside the apartment as he said, "C'mon Norma. There's nothing you could do that would make me think any differently of you. I'd even hold your hair back if you had to vom –"

Kevin stopped short because as he was pushing inside, walking toward the kitchen, he finally turned around to see a very scrawny, pale man in just boxers standing in the room... right next to Norma. He'd been just out of sight, obscured by the door.

"So, Norma wasn't even sick, she was just playing me after all," Kevin thought to himself.

"This isn't what it looks like," Norma started, but Kevin already wasn't listening because he'd decided right then and there that women were evil and he'd never trust one again.

~~~

Norma felt panicked. Obviously she was going to end

things with Kevin now that she was back with Marcus, but she'd have never wanted him to find out like this. She was all about using men when it benefited her, but Kevin had seemed genuinely nice and he deserved better than to see her with another man.

Here was Kevin, bringing her soup to make her feel better, risking his own health to do so, and Norma let him see her with Marcus. She was so angry with herself, but had to deal with the situation at hand. This was going to devastate him.

"This isn't what it looks like," she started, and as soon as she saw Kevin's face, she knew it had been the wrong thing to say, but continued on anyway.

"Kevin, I really was feeling ill when I canceled earlier. Then while I was making tea, Marcus knocked on my door," she motioned to him because obviously Kevin had no idea who Marcus was, although at this point it was a pretty safe guess.

"We'd broken up before I met you. Remember the boyfriend I told you about?" Kevin wasn't responding to anything Norma said, and he backed out of her apartment, and headed down the hall. She kept yelling after him, "So, anyways, he said he needed to talk about something important, and then one thing led to another. I guess there's no easy way to say this, but we're back together."

As long as she started and ended on a truthful note, Norma figured all that fluff in between didn't really matter that much.

Kevin stopped and looked back at her. His face went through a range of emotions so quickly that Norma couldn't even read them all. He was shocked, hurt, offended, and everything in between, and he was essentially frozen in place.

"Are you okay?" Norma said after a few seconds.

Kevin just shook his head, dropped the flowers and food on the ground, and left without a word.

Norma waited until he'd left the hall, looking like a sad puppy dog. Then she went over, picked up the to-go food and flowers. She took a deep inhale of the floral fragrance, then went back to her apartment and locked the door behind her. "Well, I guess we don't have to worry about what we're doing for dinner," she said to Marcus, with a smile.

~~~

Milton was about as bad at confrontation as a person could be. This whole time, he'd just been standing in the background, in awe at how Norma was handling this situation with grace and charm. He made so many mental notes that he fully intended to write down later on in the journal. But not too many because he wasn't quite ready for it to end yet, now that all of this excitement was happening, and he was only a page away.

Even though Milton had seen him before, it was still hard for Milton to look at what a handsome man Kevin was up close. He was even more stunning than from far away. Perfectly tanned with muscles so big that you could see them through his shirt. Kevin was the opposite from himself in every way.

Norma must really love Milton if she was shooing away this Greek god in favor of his scrawny, pale self. After Kevin silently left, Milton had no idea how he was going to romance-up the mood again, but he didn't have to. Norma did it for him by making the joke about dinner. Even though it was a rival male who had brought the food, soup sounded pretty damn good. He joined her in the kitchen as they sat on the counter, splitting the sandwich and sharing the soup right out of the container.

For a brief moment, Milton felt like this was the best friend that he'd never had, but that he'd longed for his whole life. But in that same instant, he had an unpleasant revelation: Before, keeping a journal on Norma had been the problem, but now the problem was that the journal was going to end.

Norma was under the impression that she would be the focus of all Milton's attention for ever and ever. He'd never fully explained the concept of the journals to her, and he wasn't going to now. But could he keep a secret that big from the love of his life? He'd have to if he wanted to continue being with her. The more he mulled it over, the more Milton realized that Norma was what he wanted for his life. He also convinced himself that he'd been following people for so long that he was a professional at this point.

"Norma," Milton said a bit dramatically, "I'd follow you to the ends of the Earth and back." He smiled, and then they both laughed out loud again.

"Everything will work out just fine," he told himself.

~~~

As Kevin stormed off, he was losing every bit of the "good guy" that he had become with regard to Norma. He flashed back to his childhood when girl after girl turned him down, even on Prom Night, even though he'd been as gentlemanly as possible to all of them. It was now that he decided he'd never fall for another woman again, no matter how beautiful she was.

In the beginning Kevin had liked Norma, but then he realized he only wanted to fuck her, only to decide that he might actually be able to feel something for her. Then, his heart was crushed in fantastic fashion, and he wasn't sure that he'd be able to fully recover.

Eventually Kevin wanted a family and to get married, but he knew he could find some pushover girl who would make all of his white picket fence dreams come true. If there was anything he had learned from acting like an asshole, it was that plenty of girls wanted to be treated like shit.

Kevin had even extended his experience into assholedom by pushing the boundaries with new girls he met, especially the pushovers.

Now that Kevin was leaving Norma's with an extremely bruised ego, he thought of the saying "It's better to have loved and lost than never loved at all," and he said to himself, "Whoever said that obviously didn't catch a woman in bed with another man." He got into his car and drove away, toward the strip club down the street. It had been awhile since he'd been there, but now seemed like as good of a time as any to return with his one dollar bills ablaze. Not literally ablaze though, of course.

"Maybe I can find a nice girl there to take home," Kevin thought to himself, laughing at the thought. Clearly everyone performing at the strip club had daddy issues, or some very expensive schooling to pay for, or both, but either way he was able to fix their problem. He could feign love and already had a ton of cash in-hand; the longer he thought about it, a stripper might be the way to go after all. Not a daytime stripper though. There's a reason that they're only on stage during the day.

Making his way down the street, Kevin was doing his best to push Norma from his mind, and it was working. He could now say that he'd tried the love thing and it just wasn't for him. He needed to sow his wild oats and be the man in a relationship. It wasn't possible to be the man if he was in love with someone. The real love, the kind he'd thought he could have had for Norma. That made him soft and vulnerable, which were things told himself he'd never be again.

The further he drove from Norma's the better he felt.

Eventually, Kevin knew this pain would go away and he'd be just fine.

~~~

Norma couldn't have been happier. If there was a cloud ten, she was on it. She now had a man in Marcus who loved her so much to the point of obsession. He literally couldn't get enough of her. "Because why else," she thought to herself, "would a man follow someone around all day?" She thought about asking him how he handled the time away from her, but then thought it was best to let things be rather than open up old wounds.

As they sat, eating the soup and grilled cheese, Norma began to think beyond just their relationship now. She gazed at Marcus and really could truly see herself with him.

How wonderful it would be to have an audience at all times, just watching you, your every move, because they needed your entertainment to add value to their lives. Before Norma, Marcus was so *boring*, peeking over newspapers at coffee shops, looking at strangers. Now he'd actually have a real life drama to watch, and he'd even have inside knowledge because he was a part of it. And she'd never know when he was watching so she'd have to be on her toes at all times. This was perfection!

The best part was that when they were together, Marcus was like Norma's best friend. He let her lead the conversation and talk about whatever it was that was on her mind.

They were going to be the happiest people on Earth.

~~~

The next morning, Milton kissed Norma on the forehead as she slept, and he crept out of the house. He knew that she was only pretending to be asleep, but it didn't matter because he was there with her.

It had been a crazy 24 hours, so he needed to go home, shower, and get his things together, since she had thrown out everything in her apartment that belonged to him.

On the drive, Milton started to assess the current situation. He couldn't have been more thrilled to be back with Norma. Truly. He was over the moon that she would take him back, even knowing about his inclinations and compulsions.

Now there was a bigger issue to deal with: the journal on Norma was almost finished, and Milton wasn't sure what he was going to do afterward. He could always start a new one following Norma again, but that would make all of his others seem silly. He'd ended so many in the middle of a crisis that it was wrong to let one story finish while others had been cut short.

"But isn't this the story of my life too?" Milton thought to himself.

Of course it was, but that still wasn't enough justification for him to start another journal on Norma. The whole reason Milton did this was to get a better glimpse of humanity as a whole. He wanted to see as many different kinds of people as he could, in their natural habitats. It was the scientist in him, the explorer he never got to be.

Milton loved seeing how different a suburban mother's life was from an aspiring actress' and yet how similar the actress was to the young girl with no direction in her life. Everyone was connected in some way or another, and yet so many of them went to bed at night feeling alone.

Mainly Milton had observed people of all kinds were all just looking to be loved, by any means necessary. Sometimes that meant having an affair, and sometimes it meant doing drugs and drinking as a way to cope. By realizing this, Milton decided that he'd be with Norma for as long as she'd have him, but he wouldn't open another journal on her.

It was time to move on and see what other people were like, and how their lives related to other people, how this world was somehow connected.

There was also the issue of what to do with his family home and all of the journals he'd stored up. Surely if Norma ever saw them, she'd want to read them and would be particularly curious about her own; nothing good could come of that. However, since Milton had decided to continue on with other people, there was the risk that she'd find out he was following subjects besides her.

Milton thought long and hard about how to deal with this, and finally came up with a solution he thought would work.

Obviously at some point, Milton figured that Norma would want to go get married, have kids, and raise a family. Milton already owned his home and didn't want to buy another, but his was so full of junk and memories that he didn't know how he could possibly clean it out and start a new life with her. It would take time, but now that they were back together, he figured that time was something he had. At least for now.

This would also be a great way to prolong ending Norma's journal a tiny bit longer. He would pretend to leave so he could stalk her in the morning, and then go home and start cleaning everything up.

As for his other journals, Milton decided to get a storage unit and put them in there. He imagined them stacked nicely in a bookshelf, with a little couch in the unit too. This way, any time that he wanted to go in and reread them he could, even though he knew he never would.

And Norma would be happy in a new, clean home and

be none the wiser as to how deep Milton's compulsion actually extended. Driving home, he decided to start cleaning everything the moment he got there and put his plan into action. Everything was going to work out just fine.

After spending days cleaning out his home non-stop and preparing, Milton had no option but to finish his journal. So he showered, got into the car and headed to Norma's apartment. When he got there, he scanned the area then headed to the little bush that she had caught him in before. Now that she knew he was following her, there was no need to really hide himself completely. She wouldn't be alarmed if she caught him.

In fact, she might have been relieved. Juggling his house cleaning with Norma had been tougher than he'd originally thought. Since they were back together now, and she knew that he'd be following her, Norma had told Milton it didn't matter if he slipped up while he was hiding. She told him that she liked seeing little peeks of him, to let her know that he was around. The problem was that he'd actually been miles away at home.

So, as he sat there in the bush, staring at the woman he planned to spend the rest of his life with, Milton struggled to be objective in his writing. He ended up jotting things down like:

Reads Elle *magazine languorously. Pays close attention to each page, muttering 'hmm's as she reads. Looks more beautiful than ever.*

Milton was torn between being thorough with his notes, thus speeding up the process, or taking his time so he could watch Norma for as long as he wanted. Then it hit him.

Even though he would be starting new journals on other people, Milton could still pop in and stalk Norma whenever he wanted, since she was his now. This gave him the final push of confidence that he needed to finish his journal on Norma and after about another hour, Milton closed the file "on this incredible woman I am lucky to know," he told himself, "much less have forever."

Quietly walking over to his car, Milton put the journal inside, tucking it under his seat so that Norma wouldn't have a chance to find it, and then walked up to her door and knocked.

Norma greeted Milton with a giant smile, which he

returned. He was now free to love her for her, and not because he was obligated by his need to finish a journal. He was spending time with a person out of choice, and it felt liberating to him.

Until Milton felt a twinge of dread. He knew that he'd have to find someone else to follow, and he hated this thought almost as much as he hated himself and his weird urge to follow people around. It brought up his old feelings of resentment at the fact that he was born this way and felt the need to do these things.

Suddenly he was taken back to his days in the institution, and thought of every trick they had taught him for coping with his 'disability' as they called it. These tricks involved taking deep breaths, sitting alone for extended periods of time, and burning his observations.

None of these were options for Milton right now, and while he hugged Norma he hoped that he could focus on his overwhelming feelings of happiness and let everything else go, but it wasn't to be.

He quickly began feeling anxious with the need to find someone else, so he disengaged from the hug and excused himself to go to the bathroom.

Once inside, with the door firmly locked, Milton looked at himself in the mirror. The face he saw looking back was afraid and sad. He recognized it well, but hated it. He sat on the toilet with the lid closed, shut his eyes and just meditated, trying to let go of all his sadness and anxiety and just be happy.

Tears started streaming down Milton's face, because he was filed with more emotion than he'd ever been before. Nothing had really gotten to him, but now he was torn between the person who made him happiest in this world and what he now saw as a monster inside him that he'd been forced to live with for his entire life.

This compulsion had been governing his choices for decades, and now he had to learn how to suppress it. Not get rid of it, because he knew enough to understand that it was impossible, but he could start by intentionally blocking it out for periods of time. This way he could enjoy his time with Norma.

After quite awhile, he finally stopped crying, and assured himself that he'd be able to move on with his life and be happy.

So, Milton got off the toilet, splashed his face with cold water and looked at himself in the mirror again. The face looking back was much happier, with only a dull sadness showing through his eyes.

~~~

This was the first day in months that Milton was looking to follow someone other than Norma.

It was difficult for him. Everyone he saw didn't look right.

The first woman he spotted was a thin blonde dressed in a tight sweater and slacks. Milton was too nervous that he'd become attracted to her, so that was out of the question, and raised a new category of people who he'd no longer consider as subjects.

The next potential person was a chubby girl, who couldn't have been more than 18 years old. Milton had learned through trial-and-error that he hated following teens. They were boring. In his opinion, anyone who hadn't gone to college or at least lived in the real world for a while had such trivial problems. They had issues like wondering if a boy liked them, or how they'd live down the embarrassment of answering a question wrong in class. Things only the most carefree people can waste time worrying about.

Older people had real issues, like executing a will after a parent's death or hiding an affair when there's a happy wife and kids at home.

There was one exception to the rule though: teens who got pregnant were highly interesting to him, because they were forced to deal with an adult problem.

After spending several hours in a park, watching everyone, Milton settled on a particularly oblivious mother who was pushing her kids on the swing. She was one of the five women there who weren't nannies, which intrigued him already.

The woman had two kids, an older boy and younger boy. He could tell the children were only about a year apart and too young to be in school yet, otherwise that's where they'd be right now. The mother was heavier than she was thin, and she had the short, curly mom hairdo that women get after they have kids.

This would be perfect.

She seemed too unattractive to have an affair and her husband couldn't be that bright if he hadn't told her to be more watchful about their surroundings. This oblivious family would be the perfect way to get back into the normal stalking world again; one where you remain forever anonymous to your subjects.

As the mom gathered her children to leave, Milton lit a cigarette and walked to his car which was surprisingly parked next to the family's.

As the two parties approached their vehicles, Milton got a nasty look from the mother. "Would you put that cigarette out?! There are children here!" she said as she ushered her little ones in the car.

"Apologies," Milton said as he took one more long drag, threw it on the ground, and got in his car. He grabbed for an empty journal in his coat and a pen, and as the mom next to him was tucking her kids in seats, he started to write

Mom tells strangers to put out cigs, for her childrens' health.

As he put the period at the end of the sentence,

Milton was trapped in thought. This was really the end of his all-encompassing time with Norma. He'd get to love her in his real life, but as far as feeding his obsession was concerned, Norma was gone forever.

As he thought this, Milton nearly missed the family's car leaving. He quickly turned on his ignition and followed them through the city.

www.ingramcontent.com/pod-product-compliance
Lightning Source LLC
Chambersburg PA
CBHW021532250626
47154CB00006BA/2076